The
name an
covered
Knowing only one sure way to halt her body's quaking
made an abrupt decision.

Lying beside her, Shadow Walker drew the girl against
him. She turned spontaneously to his warmth, burrowing
against him to share his heat. Her body was delicate and
warm to his touch as he slipped his arm around her and
closed his eyes to sleep. His last thought as he held her
close was of her smile—and that she was right. She was
not a child.

girl shivered as the night air chilled. She called a
and hugged her arms around her. Shadow Walker
her with a blanket, but her shivering continued.

Miranda
and the
Warrior

AN AVON TRUE ROMANCE

Miranda
and the
Warrior

ELAINE BARBIERI

AVON BOOKS
An Imprint of HarperCollinsPublishers

FIND TRUE LOVE!
www.avontrueromance.com

An Avon True Romance is a trademark of HarperCollins Publishers Inc.

Miranda and the Warrior

Copyright © 2002 by Elaine Barbieri

For information address HarperCollins Children's Books,
a division of HarperCollins Publishers, 1350 Avenue of the Americas,
New York, NY 10019.

Library of Congress Catalog Card Number: 2002090318
ISBN 0-06-001134-3

First Avon edition, 2002

AVON TRADEMARK REG. U.S. PAT. OFF. AND IN OTHER COUNTRIES,
MARCA REGISTRADA, HECHO EN U.S.A.

Visit us on the World Wide Web!
www.harperteen.com

To my three young adults, Holly Settineri,

Siobhan Fitzpatrick, and Michael Settineri,

with much love

Miranda
and the
Warrior

❧

CHAPTER ONE

The American Frontier, 1871

Holding her mount to a steady pace, Miranda again scanned the sunswept distance behind her. She laughed triumphantly when she saw no sign of soldiers pursuing her across the wild terrain. She had done it again! With an innocent expression and a practiced flutter of long lashes, she had talked the guard at Fort Walters's gate into believing her father had given her permission for a short outing. She'd soon reach the Calhoun ranch to keep her promise that she'd be there when her friend's prize mare foaled.

Miranda's smile broadened. The baggy male clothing and oversized hat that was her present riding attire aside, she had learned to use the curving proportions of womanhood to full advantage, when necessary. Private Will Blake hadn't been immune to her appeal. As a matter of fact, he hadn't seemed able to think past her . . . smile. She hoped he didn't suffer for it when her father found out she was gone, but she had already decided that wasn't her problem.

Miranda's smile faltered. Her father's overprotectiveness, however, *was* her problem. Never had that been demonstrated more clearly to her than when her father, Major Charles Thurston of the US Cavalry, had refused to allow her to travel to the Calhoun ranch because he wouldn't "put her or her escort at risk on a whim." She had suffered her father's overprotectiveness most of her life—since her mother's death when Miranda was born. At the age of eighteen, she had become adept at circumventing it when necessary, and this was one of those times.

Cheyenne raiding parties in the area—Miranda scoffed. She had no doubt that the stories circulating were nothing more than the "Cheyenne fever" that had dispatched Fort Walters patrols out on countless false alarms during the past weeks. Besides, she could take care of herself. She had lived on the frontier all her life, and she—

Miranda's thoughts halted cold at first sight of the riders coming into view in the distance. Seeing her at that same moment, the horsemen began racing toward her.

They weren't military. Nor were they civilians.

Miranda gasped, then dug her heels into her mount's sides to spur him into a gallop.

The riders were Cheyenne!

Miranda awakened slowly to the steady rhythm of a horse underneath her. She opened her eyes to a world that was somehow turned upside down, then groaned at the realization that she was bound hand and foot and thrown over a horse like a piece of old baggage.

Furious at being so treated, Miranda twisted around to look up at her captor. Her heart jumped to an erratic beating at the sight of the Indian's fierce war paint—his face a mask of jagged color, with lightning bolts meticulously drawn on each cheek, and dark eyes outlined in startling red. She recalled with sudden clarity her mad race to escape the pursuing Cheyenne. She remembered her panic as the Indian ponies steadily closed the distance between them—then her moment of mindless terror when an Indian pony drew alongside her galloping horse. She remembered swinging out wildly with the rope on her saddle, striking her pursuer across his painted face.

The last thing she recalled was the rage that flashed in those dark eyes before everything went black.

Her captor looked down at her unexpectedly. He held her gaze for an extended moment and Miranda realized abruptly that the rage she had formerly seen in his eyes was gone. Clearly visible there instead was another equally startling emotion.

Scorn.

No, she would not tolerate this Cheyenne's contempt! She was Miranda Thurston, daughter of Major Charles Thurston of the US Cavalry. She would erase the scorn from her captor's eyes if it was the last thing she ever did.

* * *

Shadow Walker acknowledged the hoots of approval from the welcoming crowd that had gathered on the edge of the camp to observe his party's return. Yet his mood was far from festive as he pulled his captive down from his horse and stood her up on shaky legs. He stared at her coldly. His face still throbbing from the lash of her rope, he remembered the wild chase that had ensued after he had sighted her. He recalled his surprise when he drew up alongside his quarry and saw that she was female—only to be stunned into fury when he was almost whipped from his horse by the unexpected swipe of her rope.

With satisfaction, Shadow Walker remembered that a quick grab had rendered the girl his captive—but that thought now gave him little comfort. With light hair hanging in tangled disarray across her dirt-covered face, her baggy male clothing filthy and torn, she was small and thin, little more than a child, an unimpressive captive worth far less than the great black mare she had ridden. She served poorly his need for vengeance against the military who held his father's brother, Red Shirt, prisoner in a dark fort cell where he would never again see the sun.

Shadow Walker stared at his captive a moment longer. She was good for only one thing.

Cutting the bonds on her feet with quick efficiency, Shadow Walker pushed the girl forward. He saw the spark of defiance in her light eyes before she stumbled ahead of him, dodging glancing blows from those she passed as they made their way across the camp.

Jerking the girl to a halt when they reached the lodge he sought, Shadow Walker noted the trembling she attempted to conceal, and scorn for her faltering bravery returned. His attention was drawn back to the lodge when the flap lifted and Rattling Blanket appeared in the opening. He spoke to the old squaw gently in their native tongue. He waited for the nod that signified Rattling Blanket's acceptance, then walked away without a backward glance at the uncertain captive he had left behind him.

Major Charles Thurston looked at the soldier who stood at attention in front of his desk. His bearded face tightly composed, he addressed the young man sharply.

"What time did my daughter leave the fort?"

"Early this morning, sir."

"She made no mention of her destination when she left?"

"She said she was going to ride out a little way—down to the stream by the bluff. She said you had given her permission to go out to pick some wildflowers there. She said she wouldn't be gone long."

"Wildflowers . . . and you believed her?"

"She seemed sincere, sir. I had no reason to doubt her."

No reason to doubt her, of course, and not able to think past Miranda's smile and potent charm.

Major Thurston struggled to control his rising temper. This was just like Miranda. She had come to his office that morning, taking for granted—as usual—that he would not hesitate to assign her an escort so she could visit the Calhoun ranch for some reason that he could not now remember. What he did recall was that his reaction had been a spontaneous refusal. He had been incredulous that she would even make such a request in light of recent Cheyenne war party activity reported in the area, and he had told her so.

The major unconsciously shook his head. He supposed he should have gotten a hint from Miranda's angry response and the look of rebellion in her eyes when he had refused to relent. He had seen that look in her eyes countless times before. He should have known it would mean trouble.

Major Thurston glanced out the window at a brilliant sun that was well past the midpoint in the sky. Turning his anger on young Private Blake, he grated, "Why did you wait so long to report that my daughter hadn't returned?"

"I was relieved from duty at the gate after she left, sir." Private Blake's throat worked convulsively as he continued, "When I returned to my post, I asked the guard about her. When he said she hadn't returned, I reported it immediately."

A knock on the door turned Major Thurston toward grim-faced Lieutenant Peter Hill, who entered upon his response. The officer's report was succinct.

"We couldn't find Miss Thurston anywhere in the vicinity of the stream, Major."

"You scouted the area carefully?" the major pressed.

"There were no fresh tracks—no sign that she went to the stream this morning."

Major Thurston's jaw tightened—because she didn't go there.

Straightening up to his full, compact height, the major ordered, "Have a patrol saddled and ready to leave with me for the Calhoun ranch in fifteen minutes."

"Yes, sir."

Waiting until the door closed behind the two men, Major Thurston muttered angrily, "Miranda . . . this time you've gone too far."

CHAPTER TWO

A step outside the lodge alerted Miranda to Rattling Blanket's return the moment before the old squaw entered.

Miranda waited. She had been delivered to the old woman's lodge by her captor, where she had then been abandoned to contemplate her uncertain future. During the endless time that had followed, a steady parade of Indian squaws had come to gawk and glare at her as she had sat helpless on the floor of the lodge, with her hands still bound. Lurid stories of the fates of Indian captives had rolled across her mind in vivid detail, forcing a difficult admission. Her father had been right about the Cheyenne danger. Out of pure mulishness, she had chosen not to believe him and she had gotten only what she deserved. Her father, however, had *not* gotten what he deserved, and her regrets were many.

Unfortunately, so were her fears.

Determined to reveal neither her regrets nor her fears—and uncertain if the old squaw even spoke her language—Miranda addressed Rattling Blanket. In a voice strong with false bravado, she said, "I demand to be returned to Fort Walters. I'll be missed by now, and everyone in this camp will suffer if the soldiers have to come here to get me."

Turning toward her, the old woman responded in hesitant English, "Such words are not wise. You will suffer at the vengeance they will stir."

Relieved to be able to communicate with her, Miranda pressed, "I warn you, if the soldiers come for me—"

The old squaw replied, "I know what hardships the white horse soldiers bring. For that reason, Shadow Walker brought you to me."

Shadow Walker!

Miranda's heart leaped with fear. Stunned into silence, she realized for the first time that her captor was the notorious Shadow Walker who had so many times been the subject of discussion at the fort. His chilling war paint identified him on sight to every soldier on the frontier and his ferocity in battle was legendary. His exploits were so renowned that his scalp was wagered for in whispers by many of the men.

Determined not to reveal her inner trembling, Miranda spat, "I'm not afraid of him."

Rattling Blanket studied her keenly, then said, "Shadow Walker is a great warrior."

At Miranda's contemptuous grunt, the old woman reprimanded, "You mock what you do not understand. It is the white man's way."

"The white man's way is right!"

"The white man's way serves only the white man."

"You don't know what you're talking about! You—"

Miranda's angry response ended in a gasp as Shadow Walker's towering figure appeared unexpectedly in the doorway of the lodge. Her heart hammered in her throat as he entered and scowled down at her, the threat in his dark eyes deepened by the war paint he still wore.

Shadow Walker turned toward Rattling Blanket and addressed her in the Cheyenne tongue. At the squaw's reply, Shadow Walker looked back at Miranda, his anger apparent. His knife glinted in the meager light of the lodge as he withdrew it from his waist and stepped abruptly toward her. In a swift, snaking movement, he slashed the bonds on her wrists, jerked her to her feet, and thrust her out of the lodge in front of him.

Miranda's stumbling step was halted by Shadow Walker's heavy hand on her shoulder when they reached the privacy of a stand of trees. Refusing to reveal her fear despite the obvious wrath that vibrated through Shadow Walker's powerful body, she glared back at him as he grated, "You are my captive, to do with as I please. I *pleased* to give you as a gift to serve Rattling Blanket, whose old legs so often fail her. Rattling Blanket denies the harsh words that I heard spoken by you as I approached the lodge—but I tell you now that her denials will not spare you if the harshness continues."

Lowering his face toward hers, his war paint a grotesque mask as he glowered down at her with nearly palpable heat, Shadow Walker spat, "Take heed of what I say. I speak only once in warning."

Turning her roughly back in the direction from which they had come, Shadow Walker again pushed Miranda ahead of him through the camp. Upon reaching Rattling Blanket's lodge, he thrust her inside, then left without speaking another word.

Shadow Walker strode across the camp toward his lodge, filled with ire. The golden-haired mouse had looked up at him, her pale eyes bright with challenge even as he had felt her thin body trembling under his hand. His knowledge of the white man's language—learned by some in his tribe from a white hunter who had resided with his people during his youth—had served him well countless times, but never better than when he had overheard the girl's harsh response to Rattling Blanket. The old squaw was his mother's sister, who had cared for him after his mother's death when he was still a boy. He would not tolerate the girl's disrespect for that gentle woman, and his warning was sincere. If the girl was as clever as the white man claimed his people to be, she would heed his warning and beware.

Shadow Walker raised a hand to his throbbing cheek. The girl had acted quickly and spontaneously in her defense at the time of her capture, taking him by surprise. Despite her slight stature, she had almost unseated him from his horse. In the time since, she had defied him at every turn, despite her fear.

Shadow Walker paused at that thought. Were the girl male, and Cheyenne, her display might show the promise of a brave warrior.

Shadow Walker thrust aside the flap of his lodge and entered, then finished that thought. But the girl was neither male nor Cheyenne. She was his captive, and he would not warn her again.

The Cheyenne camp had gone quiet and still. The sound of Rattling Blanket's steady breathing filled the darkened lodge. Only the echoes of night broke the prevailing silence as Miranda lay awake on the sleeping bench across from the slumbering squaw.

Struggling for comfort despite the leather thong binding her wrists, which seemed to tighten with every movement, Miranda stared at the small circle of night sky visible through the smoke outlet above her. She remembered Rattling Blanket's frown when the squaw named Walking Bird entered and bound her wrists with practiced ease. She noted that Rattling Blanket's protests halted abruptly at Walking Bird's mention of Shadow Walker's name.

In the time since, Miranda's fury at again being bound

had been tempered by the realization that Shadow Walker suspected she would attempt escape—that he believed she had not been cowed by his threat. He was right. She wouldn't wait docilely for her father to rescue her, but she needed time to become accustomed to the daily routine of the camp. In a few days, when the routine was established clearly in her mind, she would have no trouble eluding watchful eyes. Then, with a fleet Indian pony underneath her, escape would be no problem at all.

Miranda's temporary complacence disappeared abruptly when she heard again the echo of Shadow Walker's humiliating words.

I pleased to give you as a gift to serve Rattling Blanket.

A *gift* . . . to *serve*.

Miranda's face flushed with heat. Shadow Walker had treated her as if she were less than human—chattel that could be given and returned if not found satisfactory. But she wasn't chattel! Nor was she, or would she *ever* be, a servant! She was Miranda Thurston, daughter of Major Charles Thurston of the—

Miranda halted that thought. Yes, she was Miranda Thurston, a US Cavalry major's daughter, but she knew instinctively that she needed to protect that secret well. Animosity against her in the camp was strong. She had seen it in the eyes and attitude of all who looked at her. To reveal that she was the daughter of a prominent cavalry officer who had led attacks against the Cheyenne would only deepen the hatred and cause the camp to be guarded more closely.

Miranda smiled grimly. Yes, Cheyenne ignorance of her identity would work in her favor. She would remain in the camp as long as needed to plan her escape—*but* she would remain under her own terms.

Miranda closed her eyes at last. She slipped off to sleep, resolved. She would show no fear, and she would serve no one but herself.

That was her vow.

CHAPTER THREE

"I'm sorry, sir. I have nothing new to report."

Major Charles Thurston looked up at the tall, slight officer who had just entered his office for his daily report. In truth, he had never been fond of Lieutenant Peter Hill. The man, a career soldier, had sometimes impressed him as fanatical in attitude, but he was a good officer who took his duty seriously, and he was presently grateful to have that quality in one of his officers.

Nevertheless, the major pressed, "You've followed the plan precisely by scouring the countryside in overlapping, widening circles so that my daughter's trail could not be missed."

"Yes, sir."

"And you've discovered nothing, not a trace of her."

"That's right, sir."

Major Thurston shook his head, at a loss for words.

"Sir . . . if I may . . ."

The major nodded his permission to speak.

"If Miss Thurston has been captured by the Cheyenne—"

Major Thurston bit back his impatience. He had slept

little since Miranda's disappearance a week earlier because of the nightmares that haunted him day and night. Willful little witch that his daughter was, he loved her more than life. She was all he held dear—all he had left of the wife he had worshipped, and who had died before their life together had truly begun. Miranda had given him purpose when he had believed he would be unable to survive. Yet he had failed Miranda by allowing her youthful exuberance to put her life at risk. In doing so he had also broken a sacred promise made to the dying mother of his child.

Those thoughts darkening his mood, Major Thurston interrupted the lieutenant sharply, saying, "My daughter's hat—distinctive because of its frivolous headband—was found lying on the prairie. Beside her horse's tracks were the tracks of unshod horses, all of which disappeared mysteriously when we attempted to follow them. In the time since, my daughter can be found nowhere. It stands to reason that if by some stretch of the imagination she had merely been injured in a fall from her horse or by an animal attack, we would've found some signs. Her horse would've returned to the fort or would've been found dead or wandering. So, since my daughter never reached the Calhoun ranch, where I can only suppose she was heading when she left the fort, since both she and her horse have disappeared, and since Cheyenne raiding parties were seen in the area during the time of her disappearance—I think we can safely assume that she has been taken hostage."

Lieutenant Hill's narrow face drew into tight lines. "We need to find the camp where she's being held, sir."

"An excellent plan—one which I thought we had already put into effect."

"Our patrols are searching for some sign of Miss Thurston's trail, but they're not looking for a specific camp where she's being held."

"Meaning?"

"We need to take other steps in order to ascertain which Cheyenne camp Miss Thurston was taken to. If I may be blunt, there's not an Indian in these hills who doesn't know where your daughter is right now, sir. We need to make the right contact to find out which band has her."

"I've taken *all* the right steps. I've sent a report to Washington stating that I believe my daughter has been taken hostage by the Cheyenne. I've reported her disappearance and my suspicions to all the forts along the frontier and asked them to increase their patrols and activate their scouts in that behalf. I've contacted all Indian agents and asked them to use their influence to find out where she is. I've sent details to every ranch in the area and asked them to report anything that looks at all suspicious to them. So far, no positive response has been received."

"That isn't what I meant."

"What are you saying?"

"The Indians are savages, sir. They won't think twice

about betraying each other if they're offered the right incentive."

"By the right incentive, you mean . . . ?"

"Tell the Indian agents to pass along the word that the Great White Father in Washington wants Miss Thurston back. Tell them to stress that Washington will reward whatever tribe can guarantee her safe return by removing all settlers from the territory north of Fort Lyon to the Black Hills, and by granting their tribe sole priority over the hunting grounds there."

"That's crazy! That territory encompasses an important part of the western frontier."

"I know."

"Washington would never agree to it."

"The Indians don't know that, sir."

"Do you expect me to lie to them?"

"Sir, they have no moral code. They've slaughtered and scalped and committed depredations that no civilized man would claim, and they've broken every peace treaty we've ever made with them."

Stunned by the young officer's venom and his suggestion, the major shook his head. "No, I won't do that. I won't put my daughter at risk with a lie."

"Sir . . . the greatest risk you can take would be to allow Miss Thurston to remain in the hands of those barbarians while you wait for Washington to take action. There's no telling what they've already done to her. For all we know, they've already——"

"That's enough, Lieutenant." Struggling to maintain control, the major directed, "Carry on as ordered——daily patrols in broadening, overlapping circles, and nothing else——is that understood?"

"Yes, sir."

His chest heaving, the major remained motionless as the door closed behind the stiff-faced officer.

There's no telling what they've already done to her.

His knees suddenly weak, the major sat down abruptly. Covering his face with his hands, he whispered, "Miranda . . . dear . . . where are you now?"

Miranda emerged from Rattling Blanket's lodge in the dim light of early morning. A week had passed since she had been brought to the Cheyenne camp. Strangely, Shadow Walker had departed the camp the morning after her capture——for some deadly purpose, she was sure——and she had not seen him since. In the back of her mind the thought nudged that she needed to escape before he returned, but escape had proved to be more easily contemplated than accomplished.

Miranda scanned the wilderness terrain around her, noting that the Cheyenne lodges glowing an eerie white in the dim light of early morning were pitched in a broad circle between endlessly rolling hills. Although the sun had not yet risen, gray columns of smoke from cooking fires were already trailing up into the still air. As she watched, squaws began emerging from lodges at all quarters of the camp to join the silent parade making its way to the stream to gather "living water," fresh water for the day. She knew that as morning lengthened, the men would exit the lodges to take their daily baths in the area where the stream pooled; that horses turned out to graze during the night would be driven back into the camp by the older boys; and that after the morning meal ended, the men would mount up for the hunt—or for whatever darker pursuit they intended.

Rattling Blanket brushed past Miranda to join the women walking toward the stream and Miranda frowned as the old squaw negotiated the rocky slope down to the stream on unsteady legs. She gained little satisfaction in knowing that Rattling Blanket no longer expected her to perform that chore.

Ignoring the dark glances sent her way as the squaws filed past, Miranda was well aware that animosity toward her had intensified. She recalled her first full day at the camp. She remembered being prodded awake at dawn and having her bonds cut, only to be pushed into the parade of squaws in their morning trek down to the stream; being forced to join a group of hostile women when they went out to gather firewood a short time later; and having a primitive tool shoved into her hand for the intention of digging up roots for cooking as the day progressed.

She had refused to perform any of those menial chores. Instead, when dispatched to the stream to get living water for Rattling Blanket's lodge, she had boldly used the time to bathe the dirt from her face and arms and to wash her hair. Her relief had been so great that she had returned to the camp without a thought for the way her dampened shirt adhered to her female curves—until she noticed the attention she had drawn from Spotted Bear, a young Cheyenne warrior. Her discomfort had grown when she had then remembered that it was Spotted Bear who had ridden in close pursuit beside Shadow Walker when she was captured. Something in his eyes had frightened her. The thought that it might have been Spotted Bear who'd caught her had sent a chill down her spine.

When pushed to join the squaws gathering firewood, she had finally accompanied them. No amount of threat, however, had been effective in forcing her to play the packhorse along with the other women when they returned to camp with huge loads tied to their backs.

She had simply refused to dig up roots, which she considered a thoroughly demeaning chore. She had justified her refusal by reminding herself that she was a prisoner, and that no matter how kind Rattling Blanket seemed to be, the old squaw was her jailer.

As for Rattling Blanket's insistent praise of Shadow Walker's "bravery and generosity," Miranda had reminded herself that Shadow Walker's "bravery" had been exhibited in bloody battles against her father's soldiers, and that Shadow Walker could afford to be "generous" with plunder taken from the settlers her father strove so hard to protect.

Miranda swallowed a sudden rise of tears. Where was her father? She had thought about him so often during the past week. She missed him terribly and longed for home. Why didn't he come to rescue her?

Rattling Blanket's repeated warnings rang again in Miranda's mind. The old squaw had reminded her that continued resistance would earn her Shadow Walker's displeasure when he returned a few days hence, but Miranda had refused to entertain the thought of Shadow Walker's anger by consoling herself that she would not be there when he returned. She had learned the hard way, however, that the apparent freedom she enjoyed in the camp was as deceiving as the tranquility with which the camp appeared to pass its days.

Rattling Blanket stumbled again on the steep trail leading down to the stream, and Miranda looked away determinedly. No, she would not feel guilt. She was not chattel, and she would not allow herself to be given as a gift to serve anyone.

She pushed a heavy lock of pale hair back from her cheek, felt its silky texture, and grimaced at the fleeting mental picture of her bright tresses adorning a scalp pole—for the truth was that the squaws hated her. There was not a moment of the day or night when she was free of their watchful gaze. She didn't need to understand the Cheyenne tongue to know that the squaws rebuked Rattling Blanket for not taking a firm hand with her, or that their glances raked her with obvious malice. Their antipathy increased her confusion at her apparent immunity from them. The rancor in those glances, however, was a constant warning that if she did not act soon, she might never escape.

Miranda's thoughts returned again to her father. She wondered how he was faring with her disappearance. She winced at the thought of the anguish she was causing him and of the desperation he must be feeling. And she remembered that during the silence of the night most recently past, she had been unable to restrain the steadily encroaching fear that she might never see him again.

Suddenly ashamed of her fear, Miranda raised her chin in familiar defiance. No, she would not tolerate negative thoughts. Nor would she disgrace her father's proud record of dedication and courage by submitting to her circumstances in any way.

Miranda turned abruptly to join the squaws as they made their way toward the stream. She ignored their singeing glances, her determination renewed. She would surrender neither to threat nor to fear.

Shadow Walker's chiseled countenance was stoic as he listened to Chief White Horse's sober oration. He had arrived back at the camp at mid-morning, his packhorses heavily laden from the hunt, and had been called into immediate council in White Horse's lodge. His return had been delayed by the unexpected scarcity of game that had driven him farther than he intended in seeking it, but his time had not been wasted.

Unaware of the unusual number of cavalry patrols in the area, he had almost ridden into one head-on the second day out. The patrol had pursued him with unrelenting diligence and guns blazing, but he had eluded both their chase and their bullets.

Unseen, he had then followed the patrol back to the fort, becoming the hunter instead of the hunted as he remained to observe the unusual activity there. His captive had returned to mind at that moment. He had considered the possibility that the girl might be the reason for the increased patrols, but he had concluded that the disappearance of a common, raggedly dressed, willful female could not possibly be the cause of such military disorder.

He had resumed the hunt later, when he was satisfied that no major strike against his people was imminent.

Shadow Walker maintained his silence as the council continued. The noble warriors present had begun by smoking, by pointing the pipestem to the sky, to the ground, and to the four directions. They had offered a prayer for wisdom and passed the pipe with the sun, from right to left, until it was emptied, but he had been distracted from the ritual. He had heard the squaws whispering and had seen Rattling Blanket's wary expression upon his return. The suspicion that all had not gone well at Rattling Blanket's lodge during his absence nagged him.

Disturbed by that thought, Shadow Walker resolved as the council wore on that if his suspicions were correct, the golden-haired mouse would suffer.

"Shadow Walker has returned."

Miranda's throat tightened at Rattling Blanket's softly spoken declaration. She wasn't ready for Shadow Walker's return. She had come back from the stream more conscious than ever of the animosity directed against her. The one exception had been Spotted Bear's increasingly heated scrutiny. She had taken great care to avoid him by circling the pond in the opposite direction, which had also afforded her the opportunity of a furtive glance at a few Indian ponies left standing in the nearby glade.

The ponies—so near and yet so far from her reach.

Hiding her trepidation with a casual shrug, Miranda responded, "So Shadow Walker's back. What difference does that make to me?"

"You are not a fool." Rattling Blanket's small eyes pinned her. "Do not pretend to be one."

Miranda's affectation weakened. "I don't know what you mean."

"I have protected you from the anger of the squaws

during Shadow Walker's absence because I valued Shadow Walker's gift and sought to regain in you the daughter lost to me many years ago. But I can protect you no longer if you persist in your disobedience."

"Disobedience!" Miranda's short laughter was harsh. "No one has the right to give me orders. I'm the one who has the right to demand, and I demand to be returned to my home."

"I warn you. Do not—"

"I'm tired of your warnings!" Refusing to acknowledge the fear that Rattling Blanket's words had induced, Miranda stood up and added, "I'm not afraid of Shadow Walker, and you can tell him that, too."

With those words and an inner trembling she could not deny, Miranda left the lodge and turned blindly toward the edge of the camp. She had told the old squaw an outright lie before storming out of the lodge.

Shadow Walker had returned—and she *was* afraid.

Turning to glance behind her, Miranda saw no sign of Rattling Blanket—but the scowling squaw, Morning Star, was watching her. Yes, she was allowed to move about the camp freely, but hostile gazes followed her wherever she went. She knew instinctively that with Shadow Walker's return, even that small freedom might be revoked.

A sudden panic besetting her, Miranda shuddered. Where was her father? What was he doing? Why didn't he come to rescue her? Didn't he care anymore?

Suddenly ashamed, Miranda brought her raging thoughts to a halt. Her present situation was her fault, not her father's. She needed to face that truth—and the reality that if she didn't escape now, she'd probably never get another chance.

Miranda took a deep breath, then glanced again behind her. Morning Star was still there.

Slowly, casually, Miranda turned toward the stream.

Shadow Walker's demeanor was grim as the assembled braves prepared to leave White Horse's lodge. The council had come to an end without any agreement having been reached on the latest communiqué received from Washington.

White Horse had talked solemnly to the assembled braves. He had spoken of years of battle with the white man's horse soldiers that showed no sign of relenting, and of peace treaties the Great White Father had signed and broken—proving that his word meant little when he was dealing with those he considered savages. He had not needed to remind the warriors that that particular truth had been confirmed on the day Red Shirt had gone to Fort Lyon to speak under a flag of truce only to be thrown into the prison cell where he still remained.

A familiar rage came alive within Shadow Walker. The brave and noble Red Shirt was brother to his father, who was killed in a horse soldier raid on their sleeping village.

He remembered that night well, when the peaceful sleep of youth erupted into a chaos of gunfire, slashing sabers, and fiery torches—all at the signal of a bugle call that still echoed in his mind.

Shadow Walker also remembered the pain of a soldier's bullet slamming into his back—and the appearance of Red Shirt, who then rescued him.

Shadow Walker scrutinized the warriors around him as the council dispersed. He saw Standing Elk, Crying Crow, Buffalo Chaser, and Black Otter. All were braves who had suffered at the white man's hands. All shared the same desire for vengeance, the same anger at Red Shirt's imprisonment, the same frustration at failed efforts to free Red Shirt, and the belief that the white man's peace would be offered only at a price the Cheyenne were unwilling to pay.

And all disdained, as he did, the message received from Washington declaring that the Great White Father wanted to arrange another peace council.

Outside White Horse's lodge at last, Shadow Walker breathed deeply of the familiar scents of the camp, but his pleasure was interrupted by children snickering. He turned toward the sound to see Walking Bird leaning toward children gathered nearby, her gray braids sweeping their faces as she reprimanded them sharply.

Walking Bird, who was wife to White Horse and who was harder of heart than Rattling Blanket, was an imposing woman of broad stature. She turned to approach him, her expression forbidding, and Shadow Walker waited expectantly.

Miranda reached the stream. Her heart pounding, she glanced behind her again, noting that although Morning Star kept her distance, her surveillance was vigilant. Aware that a single shout from Morning Star would bring the camp down upon her, Miranda felt panic rising.

She had to find a way to escape before it was too late.

Miranda scrutinized the area cautiously. Except for Morning Star's presence—and that of several horses still grazing near the opposite bank—she was alone at the pool. Gathering her courage, Miranda pulled off her boots and placed them on the sandy soil at the water's edge. She then shed her baggy trousers and placed them beside her boots. Still wearing the oversized man's shirt that fell past her knees, she waded into the water for what she hoped appeared to be a leisurely swim. Taking her time, she circled the pool, swimming underwater for extended periods in the way she had deliberately cultivated as a child to incite her father's panic. Never more conscious of the cruelty of her childish pranks, she surfaced each time with a covert glance at Morning Star. Satisfied that the squaw's attention was beginning to wander, and aware that she could not afford to wait any longer, Miranda took a deep breath, then dived deep below the surface.

The words *now or never* echoed in her mind as Miranda swam unseen toward the opposite bank.

"Where is the girl?"

Rattling Blanket turned toward Shadow Walker's towering figure when he appeared in the doorway of her lodge. Her composure faded at the fury in his eyes. She had not wanted this to happen. While others questioned Shadow Walker's wisdom in giving the girl as a gift to her, she had quickly sensed a depth within the girl that others did not see. She had recognized in the girl's defiance a courage that forced her past fear, but she realized now that the girl's courage also somehow blinded her. It did not allow her to see that in making a mockery of Shadow Walker's gift she had mocked Shadow Walker as well.

Rattling Blanket's small eyes filled. Yet the girl's indomitable spirit drove her on—so like that of Dancing Star, Rattling Blanket's own daughter, whose dauntless spirit and love of life had lent joy to every moment before the fever claimed her.

Rattling Blanket was brought back sharply to the present when Shadow Walker repeated, "Where is the girl? Walking Bird spoke to me. She told me that the girl has behaved badly, and that you protect her from the wrath of those around her."

"The girl is young . . . foolish. She has much to learn."

"She scorns your kindness."

"Her courage rejects surrender."

"She was warned."

"A brave heart does not heed warning."

"Then she must pay the consequences." His expression brooking no further argument, Shadow Walker demanded, "Tell me where she is."

Aware that further protest was futile, Rattling Blanket replied, "She left in anger. She walked toward the stream."

Rattling Blanket's heart sank as Shadow Walker turned in that direction.

Her breath all but expired from her extended underwater course across the pond, Miranda surfaced concealed in a thick patch of reeds on the opposite side. Furtively, she crawled out of the water into the thick shrubbery on the bank. She refused to look back as she made her way toward the treeline, then leaped to her feet and started for the horses at a run.

Morning Star's shout echoed somewhere in the back of her mind as Miranda swung herself up onto the back of the nearest horse. With a sharp kick that sent the animal bolting forward, she was at the crest of the rise, her spirits winging, when she looked back for the first time.

But she was not alone! Behind her, a rider pursued her with astounding speed.

Panicking, Miranda leaned low over her mount's neck and dug her heels into his sides to urge him on. So intent was she in escaping her pursuer that she did not see the great dip in the terrain until she was upon it, until her mount dropped awkwardly into the depression and threw her head over heels and tumbling.

Shadow Walker held his mount to a firm forward pace as the girl's Indian pony stumbled and threw her in a violent arc over its head.

The girl hit the ground with deadly impact and regret tugged somewhere in the back of Shadow Walker's mind. He had not wanted the chase to end this way. He had wanted to overcome the girl as he had once before, so he might prove to her that all effort at escape was useless. He had also wanted to prove to her that with his return her defiance would come to an end.

Shadow Walker drew his mount to a sliding halt beside the girl's motionless body. Her bright hair lying in wet, tangled strands across her face, her brief clothing muddied and torn, her limbs limply outstretched, she looked much like a white man's ragged, discarded doll, but Shadow Walker knew that appearances could be deceiving.

Crouching beside her, Shadow Walker first felt for the pulsing of life in the girl's throat. At the steady throbbing there, he ran his hands down her arms and the length of her legs with utmost care. Satisfied that there was no break in the bone, he pushed the heavy strands of hair back from her dirt-stained face and studied the blood that trickled

MIRANDA AND THE WARRIOR   33

from the corner of her mouth. He saw a small, circular cut
where her tooth had pierced her lip and dismissed the
wound. He then turned her head slowly, searching for
other injuries. The girl protested softly when he touched a
swelling at the side of her head. He saw her eyelids flicker,
then open to narrow slits—and he noted the exact
moment when her vision cleared and awareness returned.

Fear dawned in her light eyes when he then repeated,
"I speak only once in warning."

The sun was rapidly slipping down behind the distant
hills. Sitting astride in front of Shadow Walker, sharing his
horse as they returned to the Cheyenne camp, Miranda
remained stiffly silent.

She had recovered from her violent spill. Though she
did not remember falling, she clearly recalled the moment
when she had regained consciousness to find herself lying
on the ground with a blurred figure looking down at her.
She remembered thinking as the image cleared that this
Indian was a stranger to her—and that he would be considered handsome if not for his emotionless gaze.

Then she saw the fading mark of her rope on his cheek
and realized she was seeing Shadow Walker without war
paint for the first time. When he spoke, his words echoed
through her haze.

I speak only once in warning.

Waiting with unexpected patience for her to become

steady enough to ride, Shadow Walker had made no attempt to catch her horse but had instead pulled her up to sit astride, in front of him. She could not be certain whether their slow pace back to camp was in deference to her obvious pain, or if it was calculated so that all in the camp might clearly see that he had vanquished her.

Miranda saw malevolence in the eyes of all who looked at her as they rode through the village. She forced her chin to remain high despite the laughter and open ridicule of her condition. Hardly able to think past the pounding in her head, she was never more aware that her future hung at Shadow Walker's whim.

She ached. Her stomach churned. She wanted nothing more at that moment than to lie down and let the darkness overwhelm her—yet she refused to allow Shadow Walker that final victory.

Fighting impending nausea, Miranda held one thought. *No surrender.*

CHAPTER FOUR

The predawn quiet of the lodge was broken by the distant howl of a coyote, the muted drone of night prey, and a whir of swooping wings that induced a brief silence before the drone resumed—but Shadow Walker was alert to sounds of an entirely different kind.

Raising his head from his sleeping bench, he looked at the slender figure lying across from him. He studied the girl as she moved restlessly in the pale column of light streaming through the smoke outlet of his lodge. She was thin, almost fragile in appearance, her legs long where they protruded from the oversized shirt she wore. Her muddied features were almost obscured by wild, matted clumps of sun-colored hair that lay across her cheek, and her lower lip was swollen to twice its size. Through the night, she had stirred, moaning softly each time the injured side of her head touched the mat underneath her. Yet she had not complained when he had pulled her down from his horse earlier that evening and marched her through the camp so all might see who had emerged from their encounter the victor.

Shadow Walker recalled that the girl had not looked at

Rattling Blanket when they'd walked past the old squaw's lodge, and that she had held her head high despite the laughter of the children. He knew her humiliation was complete when they reached the edge of the camp and she then raced to a spot where she had retched until her stomach was emptied.

She was staggering on shaky legs when he drew her to a halt at his lodge and ushered her inside. One look into her light eyes and he could see that her senses were reeling. When she finally sat on the sleeping bench behind her, he had known it was because her legs could no longer support her. Her struggle to stand again failed, but her chin was firm when her gaze sought his.

She displayed the courage of a lion, although she was little more than a child.

The girl still slept.

Cautiously, Shadow Walker stood up. Resolute, he slipped out of the lodge. He walked swiftly toward the place where a younger brave had turned out his horses to graze for the night. He had reached his favorite mount when the animal's nervous whinny alerted him to a sound behind him. He turned abruptly, his hand moving to the knife at his waist in a blur of movement that halted when he saw the warrior approaching him.

Wary, Shadow Walker studied Spotted Bear's countenance as he neared. He did not recall the exact day when he had looked into Spotted Bear's eyes and realized that the youthful competition between them had become more than that. He knew now, however, that although they often rode together, Spotted Bear's jealousy of his fame as a warrior had become a silent menace. Yet presently, what was foremost in Shadow Walker's mind was the realization that except for the moment when Spotted Bear's horse had stumbled, allowing Shadow Walker's mount to take the lead, it would have been Spotted Bear who had captured the girl instead of himself. That fact had gained import in his mind the previous evening when he had noted Spotted Bear's expression as the girl marched past him.

Halting beside him, Spotted Bear prodded, "You awaken before the women this day."

Shadow Walker's response was cold. "As you do."

The glimmer of derision in Spotted Bear's eyes could not be missed as he said, "You prepare your horse. Do you hope to escape the criticism your captive has brought upon you?"

"I do not fear criticism."

"Your captive mocks you with her behavior."

"My captive has learned that is not wise."

"She makes a joke of your gift to Rattling Blanket."

"A mistake she will not repeat."

"She scorns our people and our ways, and causes those in the camp who looked to you as a great warrior to question their wisdom."

Shadow Walker replied, "What do you want, Spotted Bear?"

His expression tightening, Spotted Bear said, "Red Shirt remains a prisoner in the white man's fort and those close to him prepare to respond to the white man's treachery. Those close to Red Shirt look to you for guidance."

"Those close to Red Shirt respect and await White Horse's word."

"Your warrior status diminishes as you wait."

"I serve the Cheyenne way, not my own desires."

"The people laugh at you."

"Only children and fools laugh when laughter brings retribution."

"The girl causes our people to doubt you."

His expression unyielding, Shadow Walker repeated, "What do you want, Spotted Bear?"

Spotted Bear's gaze hardened. All pretense discarded, he responded, "I would buy the girl from you."

"Why?"

"Many Cheyenne maidens look to me with favor, but I find none who pleases me, and my lodge is empty. The girl is young and strong. She would serve me well."

"She has been injured."

"She will heal."

"She is headstrong and she mocks our ways."

"I would teach her the proper conduct."

"How would you do that?"

Spotted Bear's gaze left no need for words.

"No. The girl is my captive and a gift to Rattling Blanket. She will serve Rattling Blanket well."

"There is only one way the girl can be taught to serve."

Shadow Walker spat, "We will speak of this no more!"

Spotted Bear's countenance flushed with heat. His gaze narrowing, he turned and walked back to the camp with heavy strides—as Shadow Walker watched with an anger of his own.

Miranda awakened slowly. Her head ached. Her stomach was queasy. Her body felt as if it had been pounded by relentless hammers during the night. Several moments passed before she realized she was not lying in Rattling Blanket's lodge. Full awareness dawned and her gaze snapped toward the sleeping bench on the opposite side of the lodge.

He wasn't there.

Releasing a relieved breath, Miranda closed her eyes. Her attempt to escape had failed. She was no longer the captive of a soft-spoken squaw with kind eyes. Instead, she was the captive of a fierce warrior who had spoken a warning she had chosen to ignore.

He had said the time for warnings was over.

What came next?

A stabbing pain in her head interrupted Miranda's

rioting thoughts and she squeezed her eyes more tightly shut. She snapped them open again at the sound of a step outside the lodge and held her breath when the flap was raised. Her heart thudded as Shadow Walker entered.

Unwilling to allow him the advantage of towering over her, Miranda stood up quickly, grabbing the pants she had discarded in her escape attempt. Who had left them for her? Rattling Blanket? She instantly regretted her hasty movement when the throbbing in her head worsened. Refusing to be the first to break the silence between them, she returned his stare with as much confidence as she could muster. Her silence allowed time for closer assessment of her captor.

Shadow Walker was tall—somehow, taller than she had realized. His broad shoulders encased in soft buckskin seemed to shrink the narrow confines of the lodge, exuding a power she attempted to ignore as he faced her. She had avoided looking at him as he had ridden her back to camp, but now, looking up at him in the dim light of dawn, she saw that the hair that hung past his shoulders was as black and shiny as a raven's wing, that his eyes were dark and somehow fathomless, and that his features were even and sharply cut. He looked far different without the war paint that had transformed his handsome face into a fearsome mask, but she was reminded that although the mask was gone, the warrior remained, when he gripped her arm and pulled her toward the door.

Enraged that he did not bother to speak, Miranda jerked back her arm and said, "I demand to know where you're taking me."

"Demand?" A hard amusement flashed in Shadow Walker's eyes. "To demand is the right of the victor. To you, that does not apply."

"You won't get away with this! Someone will come looking for me, and when I'm found here—"

Shadow Walker interrupted, "Your threats are wasted. I do not concern myself with the retribution you threaten. I have faced the white man's horse soldiers without fear. Their bullets have drawn my blood, yet I have survived. I have also faced their deception. I have learned from it and will never grant an opportunity to deceive again."

Refusing to relent, Miranda repeated, "I demand to know where you're taking me."

Shadow Walker replied impatiently, "I tire of your demands." He pulled her toward the doorway, then looked down at her sharply when she dug in her heels and shook herself free, ordering, "Let me go!"

The look in his eye—

Miranda flung her arm up across her face to shield herself from an expected blow. She lowered her arm when the anger in Shadow Walker's gaze turned to scorn and he said, "Your fear is groundless. Your immaturity saves you. The Cheyenne do not strike errant *children.*"

Livid, Miranda responded, "I'm not afraid of you!

And I'm not a child!"

She was unprepared when Shadow Walker abruptly swept her from her feet and threw her over his shoulder, then turned and strode through the camp. She was defenseless against the mockery and snickering of passing squaws and their children as they made their way toward the stream—but her humiliation chilled when she glimpsed Spotted Bear's cold stare.

Thrust astride on a waiting horse, Miranda was still attempting to steady her reeling senses when Shadow Walker mounted behind her and nudged the animal into motion.

Her head pounding, Miranda grated through clenched teeth, "Where are you taking me?"

When Shadow Walker did not deign to reply, Miranda closed her eyes, reduced to silence by her physical distress.

Shadow Walker looked down at the girl where she rested back against his chest. She had maintained her silence as the morning lengthened, allowing him to support her as they shared his horse. He trailed her mount at the end of a lead, aware that she was not steady enough to ride alone. He knew the only true medicine for the illness her fall had induced was the rest that now claimed her. He was content to allow it, knowing the girl's injury had subdued her as fear never could have.

Shadow Walker stared at the diminutive figure resting

limply against him. To be challenged by this fragile female . . .

He considered that thought, finally accepting that the contest was a worthy one—for he knew the girl challenged him in ways others could not.

Yes, he would wait—for the contest soon to come.

※

CHAPTER FIVE

"That would be a mistake."

Indian agent Tom Edwards stood still, the expression on his bearded face adamant as he faced Major Charles Thurston across the confines of his small office. The Indian agent had responded to the officer's summons and arrived at Fort Walters as the sun was setting. He had come reluctantly, knowing full well why the officer had sent for him. He was sympathetic to the man's plight. Judging from the deep circles under his eyes and his unnaturally drawn appearance, Thurston was neither sleeping nor eating well. It was obvious that he was beside himself with worry for his missing daughter. All that aside, his answer remained the same.

Edwards repeated, "It would be a *big* mistake for me to take you to the surrounding villages without a military escort. You'd be asking for trouble."

"I don't see why." Thurston walked around his desk, halting a few feet from him to press, "My daughter is missing. Patrols continue to search for her to no avail. Scouts have been dispersed from every fort in the area. Someone has to know where she is. It occurs to me that where official inquiries have been ineffective, a personal inquiry might succeed."

"A personal inquiry—from a high-ranking officer of the military."

"A personal inquiry from a man who is searching for his daughter."

"I'm sorry. No."

Major Thurston's pale face flushed with unnatural color. "A simple *no* isn't good enough, Edwards. You need to give me a better reason for your refusal than that."

Agent Edwards unconsciously sighed. "Major, you're aware of the situation that presently exists with the Cheyenne. With the arrest of Red Shirt, the frontier has become a powder keg ready to explode. Ignoring a flag of truce and arresting Red Shirt was a damned fool thing for the military to do."

"The man has committed atrocities."

"In retribution for the atrocities that were committed against his people."

"He'll get a fair trial."

"Before he's hanged?"

"The decision was made to make an example of him."

"As I said—a damned fool thing for the military to do."

Thurston's lips tightened. "I'm in no position to criticize the way Washington is handling the situation with the Indians."

"But you want to put yourself in the same position as

Red Shirt by walking into the enemy's hands under a flag of truce."

"I don't suppose what I'm proposing would sound so foolish if it were your daughter out there somewhere, waiting for you to rescue her."

"I'm sorry about that. You know I am." Edwards frowned. "What's Washington's position on her disappearance?"

"Washington has its own priorities."

Edwards remained silent.

"All right." Thurston paused, then continued, "I recognize your position. You can't officially sanction my proposal, but you could draw a map of nearby villages for me so I could find my own way. You can advise me on the best way to approach the Indians."

"Major—"

"Some help is all I ask."

"A map wouldn't do any good. Your daughter's not being held at any of the established villages—at least as far as I can ascertain. She's probably being kept at one of the camps that has moved north for the summer."

"Meaning?"

"Meaning that it's a big country. She could be anywhere. And even if you *did* find the right camp, there's no guarantee the Cheyenne would let you know she's there. You could be no more than a few yards from her without knowing."

"I'd know."

Edwards did not respond.

"I want to go."

"It's a mistake."

"I mean it."

"All right." Edwards's frown cut deep. "Give me a couple of days to see what I can do."

The girl was cold.

Shadow Walker looked at her where she lay on a blanket in their temporary camp. He studied her with a furrowed brow. They had left the Cheyenne camp early that morning and had traveled through the long day afterward. Still suffering the aftereffects of her attempted escape, she had fallen into an extended semi-sleep, depending entirely on his support to remain upright as they rode.

Concern further knitted Shadow Walker's brow. He had made camp for the night and eaten, but the girl had shown no desire for food. Her injury had left her weak and her thoughts confused. She had begun to speak words without meaning. She had looked up at him with an unintelligible word of praise moments earlier, and she had smiled into his eyes—stirring an unexpected warmth inside him—but she had then rambled on and her smile had disappeared.

Shadow Walker touched the girl's cheek and felt the heat there. Scooping water from the pouch beside him, he bathed her face. He washed away the grime of her fall, exposing her smooth, pale skin to his touch. Halting, he wondered at the care of his own ministrations, then told himself he needed the girl at full strength for his intentions.

The girl shivered as the night air chilled. She called a name and hugged her arms around her. He covered her with a blanket, but her shivering continued. Knowing only one sure way to halt her body's quaking, Shadow Walker made an abrupt decision.

Lying beside her, Shadow Walker drew the girl against him. She turned spontaneously to his warmth, burrowing against him to share his heat. Her body was delicate and warm to his touch as he slipped his arm around her and closed his eyes to sleep. His last thought as he held her close was of her smile—and that she was right. She was not a child.

Miranda awakened slowly to the light of morning. Disoriented, she realized that she lay on blankets stretched out on the ground, with a small campfire burning nearby. She scanned the wilderness terrain surrounding her and saw in the distance sharp buttes outlined raggedly against the sky. Beyond, the rising sun shone on snow-covered peaks that appeared to touch the clouds, and further yet the outline of black, rolling hills was faintly visible—all in an atmosphere so bright and clear that she felt she could see forever.

Where was she?

Swept with a sudden panic when memory failed her, she sat up, then turned at the sound of footsteps approaching. She caught her breath at first sight of the man who came into view.

Shadow Walker.

She remembered. She had been thrown from her horse while attempting to escape and had regained consciousness to see Shadow Walker leaning over her.

Her heart jumped a beat.

I speak only once in warning.

Yes, she remembered it all—the humiliating walk through camp as she was ridiculed and tormented; awakening in Shadow Walker's lodge the next morning; their angry exchange before he threw her over his shoulder as if she were baggage, then tossed her astride his horse before mounting behind her.

She remembered that the women and children of the camp had laughed at her indignity.

Strangely, her memory became uncertain then. She remembered riding, the pain in her head growing greater with each jolting step, and the heat in her body keeping pace. She recalled that her eyelids became too heavy to lift, and that a fire burned with increasing heat under her skin.

Shadow Walker came closer to where she sat and Miranda fought back her humiliation. She stood up unsteadily as he halted beside her. His eyes narrowed in scrutiny. The first to speak, she addressed him with all the strength she could muster, demanding, "Where are we?" She glanced around. "Why are we here in this wilderness? This isn't the way back to Fort Walters."

"Your illness lessens," he observed.

"I wasn't sick. I had a headache, that's all. I demand to be returned to the fort."

He responded with a twitch of his lips, "Yes, you are getting well."

Barely. Miranda raised a hand to her head as a mild aching returned. She touched her matted hair, then said abruptly, "I need to bathe . . . to wash my hair."

Surprising her with his lack of opposition, Shadow Walker motioned in the direction from which he had come.

Chin high but her step unsteady, Miranda started forward. Stumbling on bare feet, she exhaled a relieved breath when she emerged into an area where a sparkling stream pooled. She quickly stepped out of her pants and entered the water.

Gasping as the cool water of the pond touched her skin, she walked gradually deeper. She sank beneath the water and remained there for long moments before breaking through the surface with a gasp. Invigorated, she swam cautiously, circling the pool as her mind slowly cleared. She was in the wilderness with a silent Cheyenne warrior. She did not know their destination or his intentions. Only one thing was clear: she needed to escape.

A familiar panic gripped her at the memory of Shadow Walker's relentless pursuit. How could she escape him? And what would she do if she did, when she had no idea at all where she was?

Turning toward the bank at the sound of footsteps, she saw Shadow Walker emerge into the clearing. As she watched, he removed his shirt and leggings without an apparent thought to her scrutiny, leaving only a brief breechcloth to cover him. Her breath caught in her throat as he entered the water.

Totally at ease with his partial nakedness, he swam toward her in long, even strokes. Somehow unable to take her eyes from him, Miranda treaded water as he drew nearer. She watched as he submerged and surfaced again directly at her side. She was still at a loss for words when he looked into her eyes and said unexpectedly, "We are equals in the water. You cannot escape as you did once before. Conduct yourself reasonably, and you will keep your freedom here."

That message emotionlessly delivered, Shadow Walker swam back toward shore. Miranda watched as he stepped up onto the bank, beads of water glistening on his back—on smooth skin marred only by a small, jagged scar between his shoulder blades.

Shadow Walker disappeared from view, leaving her alone in the water and uncertain of the myriad emotions coursing through her. He was the enemy, but when he looked at her, when he was so close that she was able to look deep into the dark wells of his eyes, her animosity wavered.

Somewhere in the back of her mind, Miranda recalled seeing warmth in those dark eyes when he looked at her.

No, that couldn't be.

Yet . . .

Miranda closed her eyes, but she was unable to escape the uncertainties that plagued her.

Where were they?

Why had Shadow Walker brought her here?

The women of the camp walked out toward the sunswept rolling hills nearby. Young and old, they were intent on filling their empty sacks with berries sweetened by the sun. Observing, Spotted Bear had no thought for the rewards to be reaped from the squaws' task. Instead, he watched Rattling Blanket where she lagged behind the others. He noted her limping gait and sneered inwardly. Rattling Blanket was old. She had outlived her usefulness.

Spotted Bear gave a deprecating snort. After Rattling Blanket was widowed by a white man's bullet years earlier, Shadow Walker appointed himself provider for her lodge. Still a young brave, he had hunted with Red Shirt and shared his bounty with Rattling Blanket and others who were similarly deprived. In doing so, he had added to his stature in the camp, with many saying he was noble indeed in providing for others as he had been provided for.

But Spotted Bear knew the true reason for Shadow Walker's "noble" deeds. Shadow Walker had feared he would be unable to surpass him in their youthful rivalry, so he had used the situation to best him in a way that he knew his rival could not match.

Spotted Bear's jealousy flared anew. No, he would not pretend to serve widows and orphans, and for that he had suffered as Shadow Walker's status within the camp had grown. The camp crier shouted Shadow Walker's praises. Cheyenne maidens whispered their preference for him. Children called out his name.

There was only one person who cast a shadow on Shadow Walker's image.

A bitter smile curled Spotted Bear's lips. The camp still spoke of the mockery the girl had made of Shadow Walker's gift to Rattling Blanket. All had watched as Shadow Walker marched the girl through camp to demonstrate that she had been chastised for defying him, but the people were not content.

Questions remained in their minds—questions Spotted Bear was determined to answer when Shadow Walker's captive belonged to him.

The girl's slight image appeared before Spotted Bear. Her arrogance drew him. He would enjoy teaching the girl obedience, and he would savor her submission while

proving to the Cheyenne for all to see that where Shadow
Walker had proved weak, he was strong.

Dwelling on that confidence, Spotted Bear stepped up
to Rattling Blanket as she drew abreast of him. He spoke
her name.

Her hair still dripping from the pool and her oversized
shirt plastered wetly against her, Miranda stood at the edge
of Shadow Walker's makeshift camp. She had returned
moments earlier to see the campfire burning low with remnants of a recently devoured fowl lying beside it, and her
stomach had rumbled appreciatively. She scanned the area
briefly, seeing nothing else edible in sight, then looked at
Shadow Walker. Her stomach growled more loudly, raising
his gaze to hers.

Realizing that to deny the obvious was senseless,
Miranda announced, "I'm hungry."

His gaze holding hers, he made no response.

Miranda's cheeks flamed as she repeated, "I'm hungry,"
then added, "You brought me here. What do you intend
to do now? Starve me?"

Shadow Walker stood up, crossed to a bundle lying
across from the fire, and withdrew a leathery substance. He
held it out to her in silence.

"What's that?"

"Your people call it jerky. It will satisfy your hunger."

Repelled by its appearance, Miranda replied, "Is that what you ate?"

He responded, "What did you eat when you were in Rattling Blanket's lodge?"

Miranda raised her chin. "I ate whatever Rattling Blanket ate."

"Rattling Blanket is old and her legs are weak, yet although you refused to help her, she shared the results of her labors with you."

"I was there against my will."

"Did Rattling Blanket treat you cruelly?" When Miranda did not reply, Shadow Walker continued, "Yet you treated her with little respect."

Suddenly furious, Miranda grated, "No matter what you say, I have no intention of pretending that Rattling Blanket, any of the others at the camp, *or you* are anything other than what you are."

His eyes narrowing, Shadow Walker took an aggressive step. "And what *are* we?"

"You know what you are!" Her heart pounding, Miranda spat, "You're the enemy!"

Rocked with sudden dizziness, she took an unsteady step backward. She swayed but was kept from falling when Shadow Walker slipped a supportive arm around her and drew her toward the blanket. He ordered, "Sit."

Despising her legs' betrayal, Miranda collapsed onto

the blanket. She sat in silence, striving to right her whirling senses. She looked down at the jerky that Shadow Walker had shoved into her hand and frowned as he ordered, "Eat."

"Don't tell me what to do!"

Crouching beside her, Shadow Walker gripped Miranda's chin and held her gaze level with his as he said, "You are weak from your injury and from hunger. Only a fool would refuse food when her stomach is empty."

The truth of Shadow Walker's words could not be denied. Tempted to throw the unappealing jerky back at him, Miranda instead pulled her chin free, took a resolute bite, and began chewing. Surprised by its pleasant taste, she took another bite, and another.

Realizing that she had eaten the entire piece, Miranda looked up at Shadow Walker and said, "Well, I ate it. Are you satisfied now?"

He responded, "It is your stomach that is gratified, not mine."

Thirsty, Miranda reached for the water sack nearby, only to feel Shadow Walker's hand close over hers, restraining her grip.

To her questioning glance, Shadow Walker responded, "You are not yet fully strong, and so you may drink, but I warn you now—eat while food is still offered. Drink while water is still available to you. Rest, while you still can, for tomorrow is another day.

"Tomorrow . . ."

Shadow Walker continued, his eyes dark with an emotion she could not identify, "Tomorrow you will not eat food for which you did not work. You will not drink water which you did not bring to the campfire. You will not ride if you neglect the animal which carries you, and you will not retain the freedom you now enjoy if you attempt to escape."

His game . . . *his* rules.

A sudden fury flushed Miranda's face red. No, she would not submit to Shadow Walker's threats!

As if reading her mind, he repeated, in a voice deep with promise, "I speak only once in warning."

Responding in the only way she would allow herself, Miranda reached for the water pouch and raised it to her lips. She gulped it greedily, uncaring that the water ran out of the corners of her mouth down onto her shirt. She stared at Shadow Walker as he stood up and walked to the other side of the fire. She did not speak when he pushed another piece of jerky into her hand.

Instead, she ate, more determined with every bite.

"Rattling Blanket . . ."

Rattling Blanket turned toward Spotted Bear at the sound of her name. She glanced at the squaws walking ahead of her. The distance between them was widening. They would reach the berry patches long before she, and she would need to walk farther to find the sweetest berries.

Realizing she had no choice, Rattling Blanket turned back to Spotted Bear. She scrutinized his face with familiar sadness. She remembered Shadow Walker and Spotted Bear as children. She recalled watching both boys grow tall and strong and pleasing to the eye. She knew even then that Spotted Bear compared himself with Shadow Walker at every turn, and that in his eyes he came up lacking. And she knew that Spotted Bear could not be satisfied with any accomplishment, however great, unless that accomplishment left Shadow Walker in its wake.

Those thoughts fresh in her mind, Rattling Blanket waited for Spotted Bear to speak.

His expression sober, Spotted Bear began, "The camp still laughs at the antics of Shadow Walker's gift to you. The girl shamed you in front of all. I sorrow at the amusement others take at your expense, Rattling Blanket. The girl is difficult and willful. The squaws would have you turn her over to them so they might reprimand her."

Rattling Blanket shook her head in spontaneous mute refusal, drawing Spotted Bear's frown as he said, "Your heart is kind, but your kindness errs."

Speaking up at last, Rattling Blanket countered softly, "Shadow Walker knows my thoughts. He will correct the girl in his way."

"Shadow Walker's way is ineffective."

"All will see the result of Shadow Walker's efforts

when he brings the girl back to me, and they will know that Shadow Walker's way was right."

Taking a step closer, Spotted Bear attempted a smile as he said, "I would save you from the trouble of difficult encounters to come with the girl."

Rattling Blanket responded directly, "The girl acts in ignorance of our ways, but her heart is good. She has only to learn."

"I would teach her."

Her gaze burning deep into his, Rattling Blanket replied, "The girl is Shadow Walker's gift to me. I must respect it and his word that he will bring her back to serve me well."

"Shadow Walker is a fool!"

Noting the trembling that had begun to overtake Spotted Bear, and the hatred he could no longer conceal, Rattling Blanket responded simply, "The girl is Shadow Walker's gift to me. I cannot offend his good intentions by giving her to another."

Abandoning all pretense, Spotted Bear grated, "You will do well to consider my offer, for if you do not, the day will come when you will regret it deeply."

Her voice heavy with the sorrow of the encounter, Rattling Blanket responded simply, "I have given my answer."

Turning away from Spotted Bear without allowing him the opportunity of a reply, Rattling Blanket walked on, following the squaws who had already left her far behind. But she had no thought for the berries to be gathered that day, for she knew that Spotted Bear's hatred followed her every heavy step of the way.

The shadows lengthened as the day came to an end. Having made camp for the night, Shadow Walker sat in the silence, looking toward the mountains in the distance. The red-gold of the setting sun flowed down the slopes in a last glorious display of daylight and he smiled in wonder, knowing that in the valleys there, buffalo still roamed freely, and that smaller game was abundant. It was a place of beauty that he knew well.

Finished with his evening meal, Shadow Walker glanced across the campfire toward the spot where the girl lay asleep. The strength with which she had awakened that morning had quickly faded, and she had slept much of the day. He had allowed it so that she might regain her full strength for the journey to come.

Shadow Walker scrutinized the girl's still face. Her skin was pale, but of a tone that softened in the sun to a golden hue. Her hair lay in unruly strands about her face, the heavy golden locks seeming to hold the sun's radiance even in the limited light remaining. He remembered that her eyes were large, and the color of the sky, and that her finely shaped lips formed a brilliant smile that he had glimpsed only briefly.

His gaze lingering on the girl's outline beneath her blanket, he recalled the night past when they had slept side by side.

Shadow Walker sobered. He also remembered the girl's anger when he spoke of the manner in which his camp would be conducted. She had not responded, but her expression had been revealing.

Walking Bird's words returned unexpectedly to stir Shadow Walker's ire. The girl was pale and weak now, but she had been neither pale nor weak when she had insulted Rattling Blanket's generosity and angered the camp. He knew her defiance would return with her strength, and that the purpose to be served in undertaking this journey still remained.

He stared at the girl moments longer. But he was not a fool. He knew that what had begun as a challenge to his authority had become something else, something that stirred him deeply.

Suddenly frowning, he lay down and wrapped his blanket around him. The girl was difficult. She would continue to fight him with all her strength. Yet he knew that in the end, no matter the course their journey took, victory would be his.

CHAPTER SIX

"No, I won't do it."

Miranda stood her ground. She was exhausted. Shadow Walker had awakened her at dawn. They had eaten a meager meal of jerky before she was ordered up onto her horse to continue their journey. They had traveled through another long day, making only periodic halts that had provided little relief. During that time, Shadow Walker had treated her coldly, speaking little, seeming intent on his own thoughts.

It had occurred to her during the endless sunlit afternoon as the ache in her back had become relentless and exhaustion had reached its prime that Shadow Walker looked somehow stronger with each mile they traveled: that he sat his mount even straighter as her back sagged, that he easily held his head erect as hers nodded, and that although her eyelids grew increasingly heavier, his gaze remained alert and clear.

She didn't like it. She didn't like being at the mercy of an enigmatic Cheyenne who had spent the first day of their journey caring for her, only to utter soft-spoken threats later. She didn't like the realization that he thought his warnings would cow her. She didn't like the uncertainty of not knowing when . . . where . . . *why* they were traveling.

The possibilities that had entered her mind had not relieved her uncertainties. Was he taking her to the Northern Cheyenne—where her father would never find her? Did he intend to sell her into slavery there, a practice rumored to be prevalent among the tribes? Or was this truly a cruel game he played? And if it was and he tired of it, what would he do then?

No, she didn't like it one bit, especially when he had announced a short time earlier that they would halt for the day, had ordered her to set up camp, and had then left without another word—making sure to take both horses with him. She had liked it even less when he had returned and handed her a rabbit with orders to cook it.

Miranda looked at the lifeless, furry animal dangling from Shadow Walker's hand and shivers of revulsion coursed down her spine. Preparing game had been the duty of the cook at the fort, and although her position as the fort commander's daughter had afforded her few luxuries, she had never been faced with the gruesome task of skinning an animal.

Unwilling to admit that she had not the stomach for it, Miranda looked up into Shadow Walker's unrevealing expression and added to her refusal, "You killed it. Cook it yourself."

Looking at her a few silent moments longer, Shadow Walker then turned to scrutinize the surrounding area where a campfire had not been prepared, where blankets lay exactly as they had been left, and where the water pouches lay flat and empty. He said nothing, prompting Miranda to respond defiantly, "I'm not here willingly, and I don't intend to act as if I am."

Refusing to react to the flash of anger in Shadow Walker's eyes, Miranda remained unmoving as he turned abruptly and walked away. She sat determinedly still until a campfire was burning and the game was set to cook, when Shadow Walker turned toward her coldly to say, "Your horse must be watered, then hobbled to graze nearby, where he will be ready for tomorrow's journey."

Miranda did not bother to respond.

His dark eyes turning to ice, Shadow Walker took both horses's leads and turned toward the path to a stream nearby. Unmoving until he disappeared from sight, Miranda released a tense breath.

She would play his game, but she would play it her way.

Major Thurston walked out into the late afternoon shadows of the fort yard. He was immediately conscious of the abrupt silence that overtook the area at his appearance, and he stiffened spontaneously. He saw a few words being exchanged in whispers between soldiers standing in the shadows, and he noted the uneasiness with which the troopers looked back at him. The sympathy of his men had been with him from the first moment when it became apparent that Miranda had been taken by the Cheyenne. He knew true anger at her capture simmered under the surface, that they accepted the trick she had played on Private Blake as youthful foolishness that had gone astray, and that most of his men were as frustrated as he. But this was different. The men knew something he didn't. It was as if they were waiting for something."

"Sir . . ."

Major Thurston turned toward the young trooper who had appeared at his side. The fellow's mouth twitched nervously before he handed over a folded sheet of paper and said, "Corporal Small received this message over the wire a few minutes ago."

Bad news traveled fast in a fort the size of Fort Walters, obviously faster than the time it took to reach him.

Rigid with apprehension, Charles unfolded the neatly printed message and read:

TO: MAJOR CHARLES THURSTON
     FORT WALTERS
VOLATILE SITUATION WITH CHEYENNE ON
WESTERN FRONTIER BEING CLOSELY
REVIEWED. AGGRESSIVE CONTACT WITH

HOSTILES TO BE AVOIDED UNTIL FURTHER
NOTICE. NO EXCEPTIONS TO BE MADE.
    GENERAL GRENVILLE M. MORTON
    COMMANDER, DEPT. OF THE MISSOURI
    WASHINGTON, D.C.

Aggressive contact with hostiles to be avoided until further notice.

Major Thurston stared at the missive, incredulous.
There had been no further mention of Miranda despite
his numerous communications to Washington. To them
she was just another casualty of the western campaign.

A casualty.

No, he wouldn't accept that! Miranda was alive. She
was out there somewhere, and he was going to find her.

Crushing the paper in his hand, Charles turned back
toward his office. There was no point in waiting for Indian
agent Edwards's help, or for help from anyone else on the
frontier. With this communication, Washington had elim-
inated any recourse in what he must do.

Her stomach was growling.

Silent, Miranda sat across the campfire as darkness fell
and Shadow Walker chewed the last remnants of a portion
of roasted meat, then discarded the bone. He did not look
at her as he cut another slice from the carcass and continued eating. She stared at the few pieces remaining. The
aroma wafting from the meat had tantalized her for the
past hour, and the sight of juices dripping into the fire as

it cooked had left her salivating. Her heart had actually begun pounding when Shadow Walker had removed the roast from the spit.

He had eaten one piece after another without offering her any. Watching as Shadow Walker's even, white teeth sank into the savory meat, she had become so deeply absorbed that she had almost been able to taste it.

Almost.

Turning away in time to avoid his glance when he looked up at her, Miranda pretended an interest in the shadows of the wooded copse nearby. She suspected, however, that her pitiful ruse could fool no one—especially when her stomach rumbled again, too loudly to be ignored.

But Shadow Walker did ignore it, and she was silently enraged. If he thought she would beg him for something to eat, he was badly mistaken. She'd starve first!

Determined, she reached for the water pouch—anything to quiet her traitorous stomach. She drew back when he leaned over and snatched it back from her grasp without a word.

No food, no water.

Well, he couldn't stop her from going to the stream to get her own water.

Pulling herself to her feet, Miranda started down the path toward the stream, her step slowing as the shadows closed in to obscure the trail. Glancing upward, she realized that the moon had slipped behind a bank of clouds, and her frustration mounted. Stumbling forward, she stepped on a sharp stone and bit back a groan when it pierced the sole of her bare foot. She walked a few more feet, then stepped on something that was cold and slimy. Gasping aloud, she jumped back, then glanced behind her, grateful there was no movement at the campfire and Shadow Walker had not heard her.

An arm outstretched in front of her to avoid contact with any unseen obstacles, her heart pounding at the rustling sounds in the darkness, Miranda continued walking forward. Reaching the stream at last, she knelt down to scoop water into her mouth. She gulped it greedily, then spat it out again when her mouth was filled with grit.

Sitting back on her heels, Miranda felt tears brimming.

Suddenly furious with her tears, she brushed them away and stood. No, she wasn't going to let one dark, hungry night defeat her. She'd show him!

Arms again outstretched, she stumbled back up the trail toward the camp. Her throat choking tight with relief when the campfire came into view, she stopped to assume full control of her emotions, then walked back to her blanket with a confident stride.

Deliberately averting her gaze when Shadow Walker removed the remaining meat from the fire, Miranda held her breath. Surely he would offer her some.

Out of the corner of her eye, she watched as Shadow Walker wrapped the meat carefully in a cloth and stored it nearby. Hunger gnawing, she saw him lie down and pull his blanket around him. She waited as minutes passed. Incredulous, she realized he was already asleep!

Furious, she pulled her blanket up over her head and closed her eyes . . . hoping he wouldn't hear the continued rumbling of her stomach.

The girl was hungry.

His eyes closed, his back turned to the pale-haired female lying across the fire, Shadow Walker heard the angry complaining of her stomach that would not cease. He remembered the look on her face as the meat had cooked and the aroma had begun filling the clearing. The day had been long and wearying. Dried jerky had filled the emptiness of their stomachs as they had traveled, but it had left a desire for more. Yet the girl's unyielding attitude when they'd halted for the night had determined what had followed.

He had hunted the game, prepared it, then lit a fire to cook it. He had watered the horses and hobbled them nearby to graze. He had prepared the camp for the night to come—all while the girl had silently watched, unwilling to contribute to the camp.

It had not escaped his notice that although she had sat silently through his labors, she had obviously enjoyed the realization that a simple refusal had freed her from chores which he had then assumed. Her enjoyment had ended, however, when the meat was ready to be eaten.

In truth, his enjoyment in satiating his hunger had suffered with knowing that the girl's stomach remained empty. Bound to his word, he had also halted her attempt to drink from the water pouch, aware that she was thirsty. He had not looked up when she'd started toward the stream, but he had watched her covertly. He had heard her stumble, then gasp, and he had barely restrained a compulsion to rush to her side. He had listened to her faltering step on the way to the stream, then to her violent rejection of the water she drank. And he had heard her revealing hesitation before she'd walked boldly back into camp.

Lessons hard learned.

And there were more to come.

He had not taken into account, however, that the difficult lessons the girl would be taught might be painful for him as well.

Shadow Walker closed his eyes, again feigning sleep. Despite himself, he wondered what it would be like to have this golden-haired girl look at him without hatred, for her defiance to be assuaged, for her to smile at him in the way she had smiled only briefly.

But the girl was angry. She wanted to return to her people. She believed she would find a way to escape, although he knew she would not. When he was ready, he would bring her back to the Cheyenne camp to serve Rattling Blanket freely, as he had promised, and there she would stay. She was his captive, a gift to an old woman who was deserving.

Yet somehow she was something more.

That thought settled uncomfortably inside him as Shadow Walker willed himself to sleep in preparation for the day to come.

❧

CHAPTER SEVEN

Miranda whispered a soft, unintelligible sound. She felt strong arms drawing her comfortingly close. She felt a hard body sharing its warmth with her as she burrowed against it, struggling to escape the numbing cold that encompassed her. She—

She awakened with a start and glanced around her. Struggling to clear her senses, she realized that it was morning, that she was alone in a primitive camp, and that stretching as far as her eyes could see was a breathtaking vista of sunlit, rolling hills against a backdrop of majestic mountains.

Miranda looked across the fire where the blanket that Shadow Walker had abandoned still lay on the ground. She glanced up at the sound of footsteps to see Shadow Walker emerging from the trail to the stream. His chest bared, his dark hair hanging wet and gleaming against his back, he had obviously just come from bathing. That vague memory . . . the strong arms that had held her and the warmth she had felt pressed against her, the gentle touch—it had been a dream.

Or had it?

Miranda stared at Shadow Walker as he crouched by the fire, then he looked at her and said, "We leave soon. It is time to ready yourself."

She watched as he unwrapped the roasted meat from the previous night and began eating. Unwilling to watch as he consumed it all, Miranda jumped to her feet and started toward the stream. She returned to find Shadow Walker mounted, with her horse on a lead.

Silently cursing as hunger gnawed sharply, she attempted to mount, only to be halted when Shadow Walker drew her mount from her grasp, then nudged his horse into motion while drawing her mount behind him.

Realization came slowly as Miranda remained behind in the camp where the fire had been doused and scattered, and all signs of their presence erased. Shadow Walker had given her a choice . . . to remain behind on her own, or to follow on foot like a chastised penitent.

Miranda hesitated, her heart pounding as she turned slowly to survey the wilderness terrain surrounding her. Miles and miles were visible to her eye, without a sign of civilization in sight. Without food, a manner of transportation, and a way to carry water, she was helpless.

This wasn't a chance to escape. It was abandonment.

Miranda turned to look at Shadow Walker's departing figure where he rode at a leisurely pace without looking back. Battling frustrated fury, she knew what her fate would be if she allowed obstinance to overwhelm common sense—a mistake she had made once before with drastic results.

Vowing vengeance, Miranda followed.

Spotted Bear glanced briefly up at the morning sky as he walked toward the field where his mount grazed. His sleep restless, he had risen early. The communication from Washington remained unanswered while Chief White Horse kept his own council and the braves argued as to the best way to effect Red Shirt's release. But Spotted Bear knew that neither the response that went unanswered nor Red Shirt's situation was the reason for his unrest.

Spotted Bear looked toward the great open landscape where Shadow Walker and the girl had disappeared from sight days earlier. Shadow Walker had not confided to anyone where he was taking her. Nor had he said when he would return.

Spotted Bear's jaw locked tight. He wanted the girl. Her face haunted dreams where he proved her master. He had resolved to have her.

Reaching the grassy hillside, Spotted Bear approached his grazing mount slowly. Throwing his rope over the animal's head, he mounted and turned back to camp. He would take the necessities for a few days' travel. It would not be long before he found Shadow Walker's trail, and then caught up with him. The girl would be his—one way or another.

* * *

The afternoon sun grew hotter. The trail grew more wild. Thirsty and footsore, Miranda followed Shadow Walker as he continued his steady progress toward an unknown destination. Shadow Walker had stopped earlier at a stream to water the horses. He did not speak when she caught up to them and crouched by the stream to drink, while concealing as best she could a thirst that had become unbearable.

Strangely, the anxious growling of her stomach had ceased. That small circumstance had allowed her to retain her pride as Shadow Walker had eaten the jerky which she had once disdained, and which she wished desperately to taste again.

Shadow Walker glanced back unexpectedly. Miranda averted her gaze, simultaneously thrusting her chin a notch higher, determined to refuse Shadow Walker satisfaction at her distress.

But her defenses were weakening, just as she was weakening. She was hungry . . . thirsty . . . tired, and she was uncertain how much longer she would be able to walk on bare feet that were already raw and aching.

Intensely aware of the slight figure stumbling behind him, Shadow Walker directed his attention back to the trail ahead. He recalled his annoyance when he first realized that his captive was female. He remembered that he had thought her a child and dismissed her from his mind, believing her worthy only of serving Rattling Blanket, whose limbs grew weaker with age. He remembered his anger when the girl had defied him, and then his growing, if reluctant, admiration for her fiery spirit. But it was the girl's admirable spirit that was presently her undoing, for as she clung to her stubborn defiance, she refused to open her mind to the error of the ways she embraced.

The girl gasped and Shadow Walker turned spontaneously toward her. Momentarily unaware of his scrutiny, she limped, grimacing with pain, and Shadow Walker's stomach clenched tight. He had eaten, knowing she was hungry. He had drunk, knowing she was thirsty. He had ridden in comfort, knowing her feet were battered and sore. Yet the girl had brought those circumstances upon herself—just as her people had brought upon themselves the wrath of the Cheyenne.

Suddenly angry, Shadow Walker remembered the girl's adamant declaration.

You're the enemy.

Shadow Walker considered that thought.

Yes, he was.

"Washington is making a mistake, sir."

Major Thurston looked up at Lieutenant Hill where the adamant officer stood at attention in front of his desk. Hill had entered his office minutes earlier, his face reddened from a full day on patrol. He had made his report, indicating that his patrol had found no further sign of either the Cheyenne or Miranda. Hill had then burst out with the statement that had caught his attention where the disappointing report had not.

At the major's silence, Hill continued, "If you'll excuse my bluntness, sir, the entire fort knows the contents of the wire you received yesterday."

"It appears, Lieutenant, that the entire fort knew the contents of the wire before it was put into my hand."

"The men were shocked, sir. They feel that Washington is too detached from the situation on the frontier to direct action here properly."

Frowning, Major Thurston stood up slowly. Hill was an aggressive officer, an academy graduate, but Major Thurston's initial opinion of the man's dedication to duty had continued to deteriorate. Growing rapidly was the thought that Hill's convictions were so strong and his hatred of the Indians so extreme that his judgment could be affected.

That fear expanded rapidly as Hill continued, "Sir, the men feel as do I, that the situation with the Cheyenne is a direct result of Washington's blunder in trying to placate the Indians."

"I believe I've already reminded you that it's not our place to second-guess Washington, Lieutenant."

"Sir, it's *your* daughter the Cheyenne are holding."

Anger flaring, the major responded, "I don't need you

to remind me of that, Lieutenant."

"She's been in the hands of those Indians for a long time."

"What are you trying to say?"

"I'm saying that there's not a man in the fort who wouldn't stand behind you if you led this command to the nearest Cheyenne village right now, to show every one of the Indians there what will happen to their tribe if they don't return your daughter."

"Lieutenant . . ."

"There's not a man in the fort who'll contradict your word when inquiries are made, if you tell General Morton you never received his wire."

"That's out of the question, Lieutenant." Controlling his reaction to Hill's alarming proposal, Major Thurston continued, "As concerned as I am about my daughter, I will not do anything that might inflame the Cheyenne into taking retribution on Miranda."

"You're making the same mistake Washington's making."

"I don't intend to remind you again that you're over-stepping your bounds, Lieutenant."

"Sir, the Cheyenne have looted, murdered, raped—"

"That's enough! I can list the depredations that the Cheyenne have committed as well as you can, but that doesn't give me leave to subvert the orders of my superiors."

"Sir, the Indians are a menace. It's our duty to stamp

them out in any way we can."

"Lieutenant!"

Hill's narrow face flushed. He sharpened his military stance as the major continued, "I choose to forget what you've said to me just now. I'll forget because I, above all, realize that the stress of our present situation here at Fort Walters is responsible for thinking that might not otherwise be considered by responsible men. I advise you to remember, however, that despite your personal convictions, you are an officer in the US Army and you are subject to your sworn oath to obey the commands of your superiors. I hope I've made myself clear."

"You have, sir."

"You are dismissed."

"Yes, sir."

Standing motionless for long moments after Lieutenant Hill left the room, Major Thurston then looked down at the neatly written document on his desk. He had composed his Resignation of Command with meticulous care the previous day. All that remained was to affix his signature.

The major picked up the sheet, then crushed it between his palms and tossed it into the wastebasket. No, resignation wasn't the answer. Lieutenant Hill's attitude toward the Cheyenne was prevalent on the frontier. Should his replacement share it, it could result only in endangering Miranda even further—or possibly cause more bloodshed than his conscience could abide.

Angered by his helplessness, Major Thurston then spat a curse at the loss of another day without finding Miranda.

Lieutenant Hill strode down the walkway after leaving Major Thurston's office. Incensed at having been dismissed for the second time by his commanding officer, he was unaware of the scrutiny of troopers nearby as he wondered what kind of man would allow his daughter to remain in the hands of savages without taking direct action to get her back.

There was only one conclusion he could reach: Thurston was a coward.

Hill considered that judgment. It was not as if he had approved of Miranda Thurston and her cavalier attitude toward the rules of the fort. Thinking back, he recalled the girl's arrogant defiance of her father at every turn. He had known that had it been his daughter who had rebelled so consistently, the outcome would have been far different from the fleeting anger Thurston exhibited. In truth, he supposed the girl had gotten only what she deserved—but the thought of a white woman in the hands of the Cheyenne raised a murderous fury within him.

The memory of being officially reprimanded for his treatment of the Indians shortly after his arrival on the frontier—by an Indian-loving superior who had upbraided and humiliated him in front of the entire company—

haunted Hill. The knowledge that the incident had resulted in the first blemish on his formerly spotless record raised a blood rage in him that he knew would never cool.

"Lieutenant?"

Hill turned toward the gruff voice beside him to see Sergeant Wallace, his jowled face composed in a frown as he waited for permission to speak. Aware of the need to regain control of his emotions, Hill paused before responding, "What is it, Sergeant?"

"The other fellas and me . . . well, we was wondering—" His scowl darkening, Wallace continued with sudden fervor, "We was wondering when the major was going to let us go out and teach them Cheyenne bastards a lesson!"

Hill scrutinized the burly sergeant silently. The man was common and uneducated, as were most of the cavalry-men in this remote, frontier outpost. Hill responded, "I think you know the answer to that."

"Sir?"

"Major Thurston is content to wait until Washington gives him permission to take aggressive action against the Cheyenne."

"What about his daughter? Don't he care?"

"It seems Major Thurston is a soldier first and a father second."

"That ain't natural. Hell, there ain't a man at this fort that ain't itchin' to go out after them Cheyenne and *make* them tell what they did with the girl."

"I know, Sergeant." Adding a note of confidentiality to his tone, Hill continued, "Very honestly, I'm disappointed in the major. I never thought to see him exhibit recreant behavior."

"Yeah . . . ah . . . neither did I."

"But you can take heart in this, Sergeant. I'm awaiting my opportunity. When it comes, you may be sure that you and the others will get the chance you're waiting for to show the Cheyenne what you're made of—what we're *all* made of."

Gratified to see by the sergeant's expression that he had hit exactly the right note to put himself in a favorable light, Hill added, "And you can also be sure I'll let you know the minute the opportunity presents itself."

"Thank you, sir."

His spirits partially restored, Hill continued on down the walkway. He did not see Wallace frown as he walked back to the men standing a distance away. Nor did he know that Wallace's first question to them was, "Do any of you boys know what 'recreant behavior' means?"

"Hell, no!"

"Not me."

"Never heard of it."

Wallace nodded. Well, he guessed he never would find out.

CHAPTER EIGHT

The long day continued. The hours had held untold silent agitation for Shadow Walker as he continued riding across the wild terrain with the girl staggering visibly behind. The distance between them continued to lengthen as the sun began a slow descent into the horizon. He knew Miranda's strength was failing and her distress grew greater with every step, yet she had spoken not a word of complaint.

Shadow Walker rode forward, knowing he had no recourse—that to show mercy at this time would be considered weakness, and all that had already passed would have been suffered for naught.

A slope of terrain and a shaded area where he had camped many times before came into view in the distance and relief swept Shadow Walker's senses. With great difficulty he restrained the inclination to increase his pace, knowing that to do so would leave the girl too far behind.

Consoling himself that the day's ordeal was nearly over, Shadow Walker pressed on.

The sun would set soon, and then they would stop. That thought driving her on, Miranda forced one foot ahead of the other.

Halting briefly, she raised her head toward the cloudless sky. Suddenly the buzzing insects were no longer a torment and the pain in her feet was fading. A strange darkness was rapidly encroaching, taking her with it to a plane where she rose above discomfort—where she was no longer hungry or thirsty, and where the sun no longer burned her skin.

Miranda smiled as the darkness abruptly embraced her.

Shadow Walker paused when he reached the wooded copse at last. It was cool in the shadows, but he had no thought for the relief it afforded him. Instead, he thought of the girl trailing far behind him, who would soon feel its balm.

He turned to scrutinize the terrain to his rear. He waited for the girl to come over the rise. His heart began a slow pounding as an eternity passed without her appearance. Unwilling to wait any longer, he unfastened the lead of the horse behind him and nudged his mount into motion.

His concern increasing when he had ridden a distance without finding the girl, Shadow Walker kicked his mount into a gallop, then drew him to a sliding halt when he saw her lying motionless in the long grass.

Beside her in a minute, Shadow Walker turned the girl over. Relief flooded his senses when he saw life throbbing visibly in her temple. He did not hesitate to examine his actions when he swept her up into his arms and propped her astride his horse, then leaped onto the animal's back behind her. He wasted not a moment when he slipped his arms around her and turned his mount back toward his intended camp.

"I'm all right." Miranda raised her chin with meager defiance as Shadow Walker stood over her, his expression somber. She had awakened in a glade beside a stream a few minutes earlier. Shielded from the rays of the setting sun, she felt immediate relief. She touched her cheek. The burning temperature there had lessened and her skin was cool and damp—the tendrils at her hairline were cool and wet as well. She looked at the water pouch lying beside her, then up at Shadow Walker. No, that merciless Cheyenne could not have bathed her face to reduce her discomfort. He had not the heart.

Unable to remember how she had gotten there and unwilling to ask, Miranda knew only that the stream a short distance away beckoned with an unrelenting appeal. She attempted to stand, but failed when her legs would not support her.

Miranda did not protest when Shadow Walker swung her up into his arms and carried her with a few long strides to the stream. Her relief when he sat her on the bank and her swollen feet sank into the cool water robbed her of speech. When she looked at Shadow Walker at last, he was frowning.

Miranda's lips tightened. Did he really expect her to thank him, when he was the cause of her distress?

Seeming to react to her thoughts as he had before, he crouched beside her unexpectedly. He waited until she turned toward him, then said, "I will leave you here to regain your strength."

Responding instinctively, she grated in a shaky voice that belied her words, "There was nothing wrong with me. I was just—"

Shadow Walker raised his hand briefly, halting her denial as he said, "Refresh yourself. I will return when the hunting is done."

Miranda's reaction was a sudden anxiety that choked her throat, to which Shadow Walker replied intuitively, "You need not fear. I will return."

"Fear?" Incensed that he had read her moment of weakness, Miranda spat, "I'm not afraid, not of you or anybody else!"

Turning away from him, she refused to look back as Shadow Walker stood, then walked to the horses. She did not turn in the direction of the sound until the hoofbeats faded from her hearing—when she confirmed that he had taken both horses with him.

Both horses.

Frustrated beyond measure, Miranda leaned forward

to splash the cool water on her legs, then on her face and hands. She stopped when she remembered that he had ordered her to refresh herself. Realizing that she was again allowing rebellion to overwhelm common sense, she continued with her bath.

Daylight had faded in the silent camp, but despite her exhaustion, Miranda had no inclination to sleep. Partially responsible, she was certain, was the mouth-watering aroma rising from the prairie chicken that Shadow Walker had brought back from the hunt earlier, and the responsive gurgling of her stomach.

Uncertain whether she had simply been hesitant to walk on the sandy soil after her painful efforts to remove every particle of dirt from her badly cut feet, or whether she had not yet been ready to face the confrontation that another night around the campfire would bring, she had still been sitting at the edge of the stream when Shadow Walker returned. Realizing she might have dozed, she could recall only looking up suddenly to see Shadow Walker standing over her. Before she could say a word, he had swung her up into his arms and deposited her on a blanket beside a campfire that was already blazing. On the blanket lay a large piece of jerky.

She had eaten the jerky without a word of inquiry or thanks while watching Shadow Walker work silently around the camp—preparing the fowl for cooking, settling the horses for the night, replenishing the water sacks, all with a soundless step that seemed somehow unnatural for a man of his powerful size.

But Shadow Walker had finished his chores, and the remote, safe distance that had been established during the silence disappeared when Shadow Walker started directly toward her.

Miranda's heart was pounding when Shadow Walker crouched beside her. His sober face was level with hers, allowing her a rare moment to study the clear, pure symmetry of features that were sharp and strong before he removed a pouch from his belt, then took one of her bruised feet into his hands.

Miranda attempted to jerk back her foot, but Shadow Walker held it fast as she demanded, "What are you doing?"

Shadow Walker looked up at her briefly, his dark eyes void of anger. Maintaining his silence, he examined her foot before dipping his finger into the pouch to spread a clear salve on the lacerated skin.

Relief was instantaneous.

In response to her silent question, Shadow Walker responded, "This medicine was prepared by Running Elk, whose knowledge of healing is well known."

Miranda made no attempt to keep the anger from her tone when she replied, "First you cause the injury, then you try to heal it. That doesn't make sense to me."

"You are mistaken. I did not cause these wounds."

"Didn't you? It wasn't my idea to walk for miles in the wilderness with bare feet."

"You were warned."

"I was *threatened*, not warned."

"You were asked to contribute to the camp, just as you were expected to contribute to the lodge of Rattling Blanket, a woman who shared equally with you although you would not respond in kind."

"I told you, I'm a prisoner, not a guest!"

"You are a captive, one taken in honest conquest."

"You have no right to take me or anyone else captive."

"As your soldiers have no right to take our people captive."

"Our soldiers don't—" Miranda halted abruptly. She had heard the stories about the imprisonment of a Cheyenne warrior at Fort Lyon—an important war chief who had entered the fort under a flag of truce—but she had dismissed it as untrue.

"Your silence betrays you."

Miranda raised her chin and snatched back her foot. "The Cheyenne have raided and slaughtered—and taken scalps."

"As have your soldiers."

"Our soldiers don't take—"

Unable to complete that statement with honesty, Miranda saw the acknowledgment in Shadow Walker's gaze as he reached out, took a lock of her hair in his hand, and said, "This color is bright, the texture fine. It would adorn a scalp pole well." Releasing the curl before she could draw back, he grasped a lock of his own hair, his expression darkening as he continued, "This hair is not as bright in color or as fine in texture, but it is valued far more by the soldiers who wager for it."

"No, that isn't true. There are only a few soldiers who think that way."

"Did the soldiers who raided peaceful villages, killing all to the last child, *think* that way—or did they only do the deed?"

"That never happened."

"Did it not?"

"If it did, it was a mistake."

"A mistake paraded for all to see. A mistake hailed as great victories by your people."

"No, only by *some* of our people."

"Are you one of that 'some'?"

"I've never killed any of your people."

"Nor did those women and children kill."

"So, is that it?" Her heart pounding and her throat tight, Miranda rasped, "If you kill me, that'll make you feel that you've avenged the others?"

The intensity of Shadow Walker's gaze deepened. Miranda felt its heat shudder through her as he whispered, "It is not my intention to kill you, little one."

Shaken by his gaze, Miranda responded with instinctive defiance, "My name isn't 'little one.' It's Miranda, and that's what I expect to be called."

His gaze abruptly hardening, Shadow Walker grasped Miranda's chin with his hand as he had done once before. Forcing her gaze to meet his, he whispered, "You are my captive, and you belong to me."

"I thought I was a *gift* to Rattling Blanket."

"A gift she returned to my care, which I need give back to her only if I choose."

"What is that supposed to mean?"

"It means that this time we will spend together is a time of learning. It is not yet clear what it will bring."

Allowing his words to linger, Shadow Walker stood up and turned away, leaving Miranda silent and shaken behind him.

Shadow Walker returned to the fire and the fowl roasting there. Behind him the girl watched him intently. He felt the heat of those light eyes, just as he had felt the smooth texture of her hair and the torn flesh of her feet.

Small feet . . . delicate and pleasantly formed. Strangely, the ache within him had been almost physical as he had smoothed salve on the abraded skin. The fear in her eyes, so vigorously denied, had touched his heart with regret. Her words of accusation had injured him in ways he did not comprehend. The reality that another day would dawn in which the girl would bring hardship upon herself again caused him pain.

He was startled from his thoughts when drippings from the fowl touched the fire, causing the flames to surge upward, further searing the fowl's flesh. He sat back on his heels. Such were the conflicts between Miranda and him, flames that flared briefly out of control, searing them both with their heat. Determined to contain the flames and control what followed, he removed the bird from the fire and turned back to the girl.

Miranda watched as Shadow Walker approached her, the roasted bird in his hand. His dark eyes held hers as she scrutinized the sober, handsome planes of his face, unable to decipher his intent. She remained silent when he placed the bird on the blanket, then crouched beside her.

Miranda questioned boldly, "Am I to assume you're offering me something to eat?" Without waiting for his reply, she snapped, "What will you do if I try to take some? Snatch it away again?"

Shadow Walker replied, "I do not play childish games."

"No? Then why are you being so generous tonight when you let me go hungry last night?"

"Last night you did not receive what you did not earn."

"And tonight?"

"The circumstances are different."

"How are they different?"

Reaching for Miranda's foot, Shadow Walker captured it in his hand before she could snatch it back. He assessed the torn flesh again, then looked up. She felt again the spontaneous heat when their gazes met, when he said unexpectedly, "It was never my intention to hurt you, little one."

"I told you, my name is Miranda."

"Miranda . . ."

Struggling to ignore the sudden breathlessness that Shadow Walker's soft pronunciation of her name elicited, Miranda listened as he continued, "My anger and need for vengeance was great when our war party came upon you that first day. I saw in you retribution for the many injustices practiced against my people by the horse soldiers. I was surprised and angered to discover that the captive I had taken was female and young, for I had no desire for vengeance against children."

"I told you, I'm not a child."

Shadow Walker did not acknowledge her response. Instead, releasing her foot, he continued, "I saw only one use for a captive such as you."

"Really? What was that? Servitude? *Slavery?*"

"I saw an answer to Rattling Blanket's need—one that grew greater with her advancing age—a need that was not only physical, but one of the heart as well."

Refusing to relent, Miranda snapped back, "I don't

serve anybody's needs. I'm my own mistress."

Startling her, Shadow Walker responded, "In that you are correct. You are master of your own fate. Yet you fail to heed an important consideration."

"Which is?"

"That you are my captive. That you will remain my captive."

Angered by his unexpected response, Miranda snapped, "No I won't. Someone will come and rescue me. You'll see."

"You are my captive." Shadow Walker continued, more softly than before, "To accept that would be wise."

Suddenly aware that she was trembling, Miranda rasped, "Yet you say I'm master of my own fate."

Shadow Walker leaned closer, his gaze intense as he said, "Yesterday you chose your fate. You chose to sit idle while I prepared the camp and the food, then cared for the horses, and so you earned today's harsh circumstances."

"You enjoyed every moment of my discomfort!"

"I regretted that you had chosen unwisely."

Miranda felt heat scorch her face at Shadow Walker's response. She pressed, "Let me see if I understand you . . ." She took a shaky breath. "You're letting me eat now because you starved me last night and tortured me all day today, and you think I've had enough . . . but if I refuse to work and do the chores that you think I should do tomorrow, you'll torture me again." Miranda's voice was trembling. "That's it, isn't it?"

"Miranda . . ." Shadow Walker unexpectedly took her hands. She was startled at the gentleness of his touch when he turned her palms upward and whispered, "These hands are not expected to serve. They are expected to share the labors of those with whom they live."

"But I don't want to live with the Cheyenne. I want to go home!"

"You are where you will stay."

Despising the tears that suddenly welled, Miranda snatched back her hands and turned away from Shadow Walker, then heard him say, "Tears come because you are hungry and tired."

Miranda snapped back, "I'm not crying."

Gently turning her face back toward his, Shadow Walker saw the tears rigidly withheld and said, "No, you are not."

Standing, Shadow Walker walked toward the horses and disappeared from view before Miranda could prove him wrong.

CHAPTER NINE

Dawn crept across the night sky, sending a column of silver light into Rattling Blanket's lodge. Stirring on her sleeping bench, Rattling Blanket did not immediately rise. With daylight came the need to bring living water up from the stream, but she was not thirsty, and there was no one in her lodge to drink but herself. She would soon need to cook in order to break the night fast, but she was not hungry, and without anyone to share the result of her labors, she had no incentive to begin.

Rattling Blanket unconsciously sighed. She was alone again. She had been widowed and had then lost her daughter. Much time had elapsed since then, but the ache within had not ceased. She had believed she had seen Dancing Star's spirit flash in the eyes of the yellow-haired girl given to her by Shadow Walker, but she had suffered both criticism and disappointment for believing. Yet when Shadow Walker had returned to chastise the girl, and when Spotted Bear had then attempted to buy the girl from her for his own devious purposes, she had felt an emotion come to life that she had never expected to feel again.

Rattling Blanket raised a hand to eyes that were

suddenly moist. She sat up abruptly, startled by a sound outside her lodge. She was standing beside her sleeping bench when she heard a familiar voice.

With a bid to enter and a heart that was suddenly pounding, Rattling Blanket saw the flap lift to reveal Two Moons standing there.

Rattling Blanket caught her breath. Two Moons was old and bowed by the years, but the aged squaw was revered by many for her ability to read the sacred smoke.

Two Moons's eyes were dark pinpoints of light in her wizened face when she said abruptly, "Last night the fire burned low in my lodge, and the fiery tongues whispered to me. They spoke of anger and unrest that would visit this camp."

Regaining her voice, Rattling Blanket replied, "Why do you come here to tell me this?"

Two Moons responded, "When the tongues stilled, my mind was not at rest. I raised the fire again and showered it with fragrant herbs—and it was then that I saw her."

"Her?"

"The yellow-haired one. I saw her sitting her horse in our camp, and I saw the white man's horse soldiers all around her."

"No, the girl is with Shadow Walker, far from this place."

"I saw blood." Two Moons shuddered. "I heard cries of pain."

Rattling Blanket shook her head, vigorously rejecting the image the old woman drew, but Two Moons continued insistently, "I heard gunfire and I saw our people running and shouting. I saw Shadow Walker lying on the ground with—"

"No! I will hear no more!"

Closing the distance between them in a few quick steps, Two Moons placed her bony hand on Rattling Blanket's arm and whispered, "It was a warning. The girl brings danger to our people."

"Shadow Walker has taken the girl away because of her defiant ways, but he will bring her back respectful of the Cheyenne and all we wish to teach her."

"I saw flames that would consume our lodges."

"No." Rattling Blanket countered adamantly, "You saw only a dream that means nothing."

Remaining silent for long moments, Two Moons then whispered, "The warning has been given. I will speak of it no more."

Silent as Two Moons walked out into the lightening dawn, Rattling Blanket then closed her eyes.

Trembling when the images Two Moons had drawn flashed again before her mind, Rattling Blanket struggled with all her strength to dismiss them.

* * *

The early-morning camp was silent. Miranda avoided Shadow Walker's glance as they prepared for a new day on the trail, and Shadow Walker felt her discomfort. She had not slept well and had tossed and turned on her blanket through the night. He knew, because he had lain awake, conscious of her unrest.

Shadow Walker watched Miranda covertly as she moved around the camp. The strain of the previous day and her restless night were clearly visible. She was strangely pale underneath the sun-kissed color of her skin, and her light eyes were ringed with shadows. She struggled to hide her limping, but her pain was obvious. He knew they need travel longer before they reached their destination and he wondered if her strength would prevail.

You're the enemy!

Yes, he was her enemy—because she willed it to be so. Yet his feelings had become strangely conflicted. His experience with women had not prepared him for the emotions this "Miranda" raised in him. She angered him, but anger and admiration were somehow intertwined. He had responded to her rebellion in the only way he could, but her resulting discomfort caused him regret. With her light coloring and stubborn defiance of him, she was the antithesis of the women of his tribe he had always admired, yet he was drawn to her in ways that stirred him deeply.

Miranda made no secret of her feelings. She pretended no love for the Cheyenne, and he knew escape was in her heart. However, she would not escape. She was his captive. In that way—and in ways he did not yet fully comprehend—she was bound to him.

That thought firm, Shadow Walker readied his horse for the day's journey, then turned toward Miranda where she stood uncertain.

Beside her in a few steps, Shadow Walker swung her up onto a waiting horse, then mounted his own and urged it into motion.

Daylight rapidly brightened as Spotted Bear nudged his mount to a faster pace. Up at dawn, he had scouted the rolling terrain, his heart quickening its beating when he discovered the remains of a recent campfire. Looking closer, he saw the signs for which he had been searching. Two horses, one unshod, and one with a curve to its hoof that clearly betrayed its identity.

Spotted Bear raised his gaze to the mountains in the distance. Shadow Walker and the girl traveled northward, to a place that Shadow Walker knew well. But what Shadow Walker did not know was that Spotted Bear followed him.

Spotted Bear's lips curved in a hard smile. A surprise, then the moment when all would be settled at last.

The day grew hotter as the afternoon wore on. It drugged Miranda's senses as she sat her mount, riding at

Shadow Walker's side. She had not slept well, and the strain of the previous day remained. Weighing heavily on her mind was the realization that as she had tossed and turned through the night, it had not been hunger that had kept her sleepless. Instead, confusion had prohibited sleep.

Shadow Walker was her enemy. He had treated her cruelly, yet his touch had been gentle when he cared for her, and his gaze had held a heat she could not quite define. Strangely, she had believed him when he'd whispered that he had felt no joy in her discomfort. Those words had somehow touched a chord within her, and when she had arisen to the new day and felt his gaze following her, she had felt even more unsettled.

Miranda scrutinized the wilderness terrain through which they passed—sunswept, endless in scope, bounded only by mountains in the distance.

She was hot. She was tired. Her body ached and her head was throbbing. She wanted to go home to her father, to a place where she was safe from the conflicting emotions that taxed her remaining strength, and from the enigmatic warrior who was the cause of her turmoil.

What was this game he played? She needed to know.

Suddenly determined to receive an answer to her question, Miranda turned toward Shadow Walker. She broke the silence between them, asking abruptly, "Where are we going? I demand to know."

His response a frown, Shadow Walker replied levelly,

"You travel over unfamiliar ground, the captive of a man you have named your enemy. Your feet are bare, your stomach is empty, your body thirsts, and you depend on this man to provide for your needs—yet you *demand*."

"Is that why you brought me all this way, to intimidate me?"

"The truth is not intimidation."

Miranda rasped, "Let me go home. Keeping me prisoner will cause more trouble for your people than any single captive can possibly be worth."

Shadow Walker scrutinized her a moment longer. Nudging his mount closer, he reached out to touch her forehead and Miranda slapped away his hand.

With a swift movement of his powerful arm, Shadow Walker swept Miranda from her horse and settled her astride in front of him. Miranda felt his anger as he held her clearly captive and whispered against her ear, "Close your eyes and speak no more, but consider your rash actions carefully."

Miranda closed her eyes, suddenly unable to do else. She was tired in mind and body, and Shadow Walker's arms around her were unyielding.

Laundry in hand, Rattling Blanket made her way unsteadily down the trail to the stream. The afternoon sun was bright and hot. The camp had already quieted for the afternoon. The lodges were closed to outside activity while most took their repose during the heat of the day.

Aware that an attempt to rest would be fruitless while the warning Two Moons had conveyed to her that morning occupied her thoughts, Rattling Blanket had chosen instead to use the time at the stream where she would be alone, and where her busy hands might lessen her anxiety.

. . . *Blood, cries of pain . . . gunfire . . . people running and shouting . . . Shadow Walker lying on the ground . . .*

· And amid it all the yellow-haired girl.

Negotiating the steep trail, Rattling Blanket raised a hand to her head to wipe away the perspiration that her anxious thoughts had raised. She earnestly wished she were one of those who scoffed at Two Moons's power, but she had lived too long and had seen too much to believe that the old squaw's mind was faltering. The girl whose spirit so resembled Dancing Star's had found a place in her heart. She still hoped that the time would come when—

The sandy soil of the path shifted unexpectedly beneath Rattling Blanket's moccasins, interrupting her rambling thoughts. Her balance wavered. Uncertain of the exact moment when her feet slipped out from under her, Rattling Blanket went tumbling down the trail to a painful, jolting stop that ended in darkness.

Myriad emotions assaulted Shadow Walker as his mount moved steadily onward. He looked down at Miranda where she remained motionless in his arms. Her outburst earlier had been unexpected. It had shattered hours of silent travel with a bitterness that he had believed had begun to lessen. He had reacted with spontaneous anger and had demonstrated to Miranda with one swoop of his arm that her demands had no value at all.

Shadow Walker felt the brush of Miranda's bright hair underneath his chin, silently acknowledging that their brief, harsh exchange had demonstrated something else as well—for as Miranda lay back against him in a semi-sleep, her back fitted to the curve of his chest, he knew that these days they had spent together had become more than a battle of wills. He knew that Miranda felt the strain of conflicting emotions as well as he, and the thought quickened the beating of his heart.

But she was stubborn and continued to challenge him. Her present silence was not in response to his command, but was a result of a physical need for sleep that even her fiery spirit could not deny.

His thoughts interrupted unexpectedly by the sound of a whinny in the distance, Shadow Walker turned tensely to survey the terrain behind him. His gaze stopped cold on a horseman rapidly approaching.

Uncertain of what had stirred her, Miranda opened her eyes to a sun that was rapidly dropping toward the horizon, and to the realization that after brave words and an angry exchange, she had fallen asleep in her captor's arms.

Humiliation flushed her face before she realized that Shadow Walker's stance had grown rigid. She glanced up at him, about to speak, but was halted by the chilling look in his eyes. She then realized that Shadow Walker's attention had shifted to a horseman in the distance. Her breath caught in her throat when she recognized him.

Spotted Bear grunted with satisfaction as Shadow Walker turned his horse to face his approach. He pushed his mount to a faster pace with deadly fervor.

Reining up beside Shadow Walker at last, Spotted Bear felt the white heat of jealousy pulsing. The girl was in Shadow Walker's arms, resting against Shadow Walker's chest. They both greeted him with silence, their expressions void of welcome.

Not waiting for Shadow Walker to speak, Spotted Bear addressed him coldly. "You still travel. I had expected to meet up with you sooner, and then I realized the destination you sought."

Refusing to enter into meaningless conversation, Shadow Walker responded sharply, "Why do you follow me, Spotted Bear?"

"I come to claim my property." Spotted Bear's jaw hardened. "You have had your use of it long enough."

"Your property?"

Spotted Bear rasped, "This captive is rightfully mine."

"This captive is mine—won in fair conquest."

"She was stolen from me when my horse faltered."

"Your horse faltered when you chose haste without prudence."

"When you surged past me to seize the girl!"

"To fairly claim her."

"No!"

"I warn you to think of what you say."

"Your warnings do not frighten me."

His tone unmistakable, Shadow Walker said, "There is only one way that the girl will be yours."

Smiling, Spotted Bear drew his knife.

Suddenly aware that she was trembling, Miranda stared at Spotted Bear as he drew his knife. Shadow Walker dismounted abruptly. He swung her down behind him and pushed her a safe distance away as Spotted Bear dismounted as well. Her incredulity growing, Miranda saw Shadow Walker draw his knife from the sheath at his waist. She opened her mouth to protest, but no sound emerged as the two warriors began circling in menacing postures— their gazes intent and their knives tightly clenched.

Spotted Bear lashed out at Shadow Walker in a sudden, lightning-fast movement that caught Miranda's breath. Her heart pounded as Shadow Walker jumped back, agilely dodging the attack and reciprocating with a thrust of his own. Striking out again and again, Spotted Bear slashed the air with deadly intent, while Shadow Walker countered with quick, jabbing lunges that Spotted Bear avoided.

Her mind freezing with sudden horror, Miranda saw Spotted Bear lunge unexpectedly, his knife creasing Shadow Walker's arm to draw first blood. She saw the flash of triumph on Spotted Bear's face and her stomach convulsed with fear as blood dripped from Shadow Walker's wound.

Ignoring his injury as Spotted Bear pressed forward, Shadow Walker avoided one thrust, then another, his wounded arm springing up again and again in slashing response.

Mesmerized by the deadly dance enacted before her eyes, Miranda realized that although she had been unaware of the rivalry between the two warriors, her instinctive reaction to Spotted Bear had been correct. She knew just as instinctively that Spotted Bear's accusations were untrue, that Spotted Bear had no true claim to her or the honor among his peers that Shadow Walker possessed. She sensed with growing dread what Shadow Walker's defeat at Spotted Bear's hands could bring.

Perspiration beading their foreheads, the warriors charged more violently, thrusting with greater fervor. The circling ended unexpectedly in a violent crash of bodies that sent the warriors tumbling and rolling, locked in a struggle that could end in only one way.

Miranda gasped with fear as Shadow Walker was thrown to his back with Spotted Bear atop him, as

Spotted Bear's knife descended with deadly accuracy toward Shadow Walker's throat. In a flash of movement too quick for the eye, the roles were reversed, with Shadow Walker knocking the knife from Spotted Bear's hand as he emerged atop his snarling opponent.

Wide-eyed with terror, Miranda covered her mouth as Shadow Walker's knife rapidly descended. The tip of his blade nicked Spotted Bear's throat, but stopped abruptly before the mortal thrust.

Hardly daring to breathe, Miranda heard Shadow Walker whisper, "Your life is mine, Spotted Bear."

His gaze fixed on the knife at his throat, Spotted Bear made no reply as Shadow Walker continued, "Your blood trails from the tip of my blade, and your breath hangs in the balance . . . but it is not my desire to strike a fatal wound. The choice is yours. I would hear you relinquish your claim to the girl, once and for all, so this dispute might not leave the Cheyenne nation with one less warrior to defend its honor."

Breathing heavily, Shadow Walker paused, then pressed, "I would hear you say those words *now*, Spotted Bear."

An eternity of silence passed in the moment before Spotted Bear responded with a hardly discernible nod of agreement.

Shadow Walker commanded, "I would hear you *speak* the words, Spotted Bear."

Another eternity, then Spotted Bear's rasping reply: "The girl is yours."

Stepping back, Shadow Walker allowed Spotted Bear to rise. He watched with unrelenting caution as Spotted Bear turned to his horse, then mounted. Maintaining his guard until the vanquished warrior rode out of sight, Shadow Walker remounted. With blood still dripping from his wound, he swept Miranda up astride in front of him and nudged his mount into motion.

Laughing and shouting, their bodies bared to the heat of late afternoon, the children of the Cheyenne camp ran down the trail toward the shaded pool with indulgent squaws following. Startled when the children's laughter suddenly became frightened cries, the squaws raced forward, only to stop still in shock at the sight of Rattling Blanket lying bloodied and still at the bottom of the trail.

CHAPTER TEN

Shadow Walker turned his mount toward a grove of trees nearby, then drew it to a halt in the shadows. The setting sun had signaled an end to the eventful day's travel, but Shadow Walker had pressed onward until daylight was failing.

Glancing down at the ragged slash on Shadow Walker's forearm, Miranda swallowed tightly. Shadow Walker had kept his silence about Spotted Bear's unexpected appearance and had ignored the blood that dripped from his wound. She wondered what he was thinking—then questioned her own thoughts as well. She remembered her fear as the violence between Spotted Bear and Shadow Walker escalated, recalling the true sense of rage that had overwhelmed her when Spotted Bear's knife had creased Shadow Walker's skin.

Looking down at Shadow Walker as he dismounted, Miranda glimpsed in his eyes a dark determination that she had not seen before. She started to dismount, only to have Shadow Walker swing her to the ground with no sign of debility.

Unable to hold her silence any longer, Miranda said,

"Your arm is still bleeding. You should care for it before the wound becomes poisoned."

Unexpectedly locking her gaze with his, Shadow Walker responded, "Would you have said the same to Spotted Bear if he had been the victor?"

Startled by the question, Miranda hesitated. Her silence turned Shadow Walker with a knowing glance toward a stream in the shadows of the glade. She watched as he knelt beside it and lowered his arm into the water.

Following, hardly aware of her intent, Miranda knelt beside him. She saw Shadow Walker wince as the water raised blood from his wound, and her response came with a sincerity straight from the heart when she said, "No, I wouldn't have said the same thing to Spotted Bear."

Turning toward her with unexpected heat, Shadow Walker grated, "More blood would need be shed than this which now trails from my wound before I would allow anyone to claim what is mine."

Frowning at his response, Miranda was about to rise when she saw the pool beneath Shadow Walker's arm reddening. The wound was ragged and deep. It continued to bleed. She muttered, "Doc Blandis would probably say that cut needs to be stitched."

Shadow Walker's dark eyes snapped up to hers. "I have suffered greater wounds than this. It will heal as the others did."

"It's bleeding again."

Holding her gaze, Shadow Walker replied, "It is only Cheyenne blood. Your people shed it easily."

Suddenly angry, Miranda responded, "It wasn't a white horse soldier's knife that cut your arm."

"No, it was not."

Shadow Walker frowned. He lowered his arm into the water again, then stood up.

Unable to ignore the free-flowing wound, Miranda stood up beside him and pressed, "You have to stop the bleeding. Don't you have anything to bind it up with?"

A new note entered Shadow Walker's tone when he asked, "Are you concerned about my welfare, Miranda?"

Annoyed, Miranda responded, "If you mean by that would I enjoy seeing you bleed to death—no, I wouldn't."

"Why? I hold you captive. If I were to bleed to death, you would be able to escape."

"Would I . . . in this wilderness? I don't even know where we are."

"So, you wish to see me survive because *you* wish to survive."

Miranda did not respond.

"Or is it something else?" Shadow Walker moved a step closer. When Miranda did not respond, Shadow Walker pressed, "Tell me, Miranda."

Struggling against the unexplained emotions that Shadow Walker's nearness evoked, Miranda responded tightly, "The answer is simple. I don't like Spotted Bear. There's a cruelty in him that . . . well . . . I don't see in you."

"Yet you have called me cruel."

"You're not like him."

"No?" Shadow Walker pressed, "How much less cruel am I, when I ate and left you hungry . . . when I drank and left you thirsty . . . when I rode as you walked with feet that were cut and bleeding?"

"That was different."

"How was it different, Miranda?"

"Because it was."

"Tell me."

The intensity of Shadow Walker's tone raised a new quivering inside Miranda. His gaze demanded an honesty she could not deny as she said, "Because, however everything turned out, you didn't act out of a desire to hurt me."

"I didn't?"

"No."

"What was my reasoning, then?"

"You know very well what your reasoning was. You wanted to teach me a lesson!" Grateful for the sudden anger that swept more confusing emotions from her mind, Miranda continued, "But I don't need anyone to teach me that you'll bleed yourself dry if you don't fix that wound."

Shadow Walker returned, "Would that really disturb you, Miranda?"

"Yes, it would."

"Because you need me in order to survive in this wilderness?"

"Because . . . because it would be inhumane to watch a person bleed to death."

Shadow Walker's gaze hardened. "You need not concern yourself. Cheyenne blood is easily spent."

"Oh, stop this, will you?" Suddenly unwilling to continue their verbal sparring any longer, Miranda urged, "Look at your arm! The cut is deep. It needs to be tended to."

Studying her expression for a silent moment, Shadow Walker conceded, "I have medicine that will heal this wound."

"Get it, then, so we can take care of your arm."

"My arm is not a concern. A campfire must be lit and the camp readied for the night before darkness falls."

"But—"

Cutting short her response, Shadow Walker turned back toward the horses.

Spotted Bear glanced up at the darkening sky, his face grimly set as he rode steadily onward. Animosity a tight knot within him, he recalled his confrontation with Shadow Walker earlier that day. He touched the nick on his throat—a small, barely noticeable piercing of the skin where Shadow Walker's knife had held his life in the balance. His humiliation heightened by the knowledge that the girl was witness to his debasement, he had been tempted to sacrifice his life rather than allow Shadow Walker victory, but his hatred had been too intense to let the contest between them end there.

Burned into Spotted Bear's memory was the girl's expression when he drew himself to his feet from under Shadow Walker's blade, when she moved spontaneously to stand at Shadow Walker's side. Those few steps significant, he had vowed at that moment that the day would come when the girl would move as spontaneously to his side— out of loyalty or fear, he did not care. His victory then complete, he would flaunt the girl in front of Shadow Walker and before all the camp, so that all who stood witness would know Shadow Walker's true worth.

Spotted Bear sneered. He would pause to hunt before returning to the Cheyenne camp. He would then enter with his mount heavily loaded with game so no one need suspect the reason for his absence. Shadow Walker—noble as he was—would keep his silence about their encounter. As for the girl, he would see to it that she would eventually pay heavily for any unwise words she chose to speak upon their return.

A hint of a smile touching his lips for the first time, Spotted Bear indulged thoughts of the punishment lying in wait for the girl should that occasion come to pass.

His expression sobering when that enjoyment paled,

Spotted Bear contemplated Shadow Walker's image and the dark vengeance that would eventually be his.

The campfire burned brightly in the darkness and the blankets had been set for the night. Seated beside Shadow Walker on his sleeping blanket, Miranda held the medicine pouch in her hand as she examined his wound.

Silent, Shadow Walker studied Miranda as well. She wore an expression of concern that he knew was not feigned as her delicate fingers gently explored the wounded area of his arm, and he wondered at the change that a few short hours had made.

With the events of that afternoon returning in a rush, Shadow Walker remembered the fierce emotions that had surged within him when he'd seen Spotted Bear approaching. He had felt his fingers itch for the knife at his waist when Spotted Bear looked at Miranda—yet he had waited.

He had not needed to wait long.

A blood rage had suffused his senses when Spotted Bear had made claim to Miranda. His blade had ached to taste Spotted Bear's flesh, but when it was poised for the task, a nagging honor had forced him to offer Spotted Bear his life.

It was only when Spotted Bear had disappeared from view and he had swept Miranda up onto his horse—when his arms had closed around her again—that he recognized the true motivation for the fury that had overwhelmed him. Miranda belonged to him in ways that he'd just begun to comprehend.

Miranda looked up at him, interrupting his thoughts when she said, "You're so stubborn. You should've let me tend to this wound earlier. As it is, you'll probably have a terrible scar when it heals."

"The scars of battles waged and won are proudly worn."

"Really?" Miranda shook her head. "That's another difference between your people and mine."

"The differences are not so great. The horse soldiers are given badges of metal for each wound received and each battle won. They wear them with honor, no matter how dishonorably they are achieved."

"Dishonorably?" Miranda stiffened. "Our cavalry fights with honor."

"By killing women and children in their sleep?"

"War is cruel and inhuman. It demands a high price from those who wage it."

"Dead women and children are not easily forgotten."

Miranda's light eyes searched his. Shadow Walker felt their probing heat settle deep inside him when she responded at last, "No, I suppose they aren't."

Her gaze abandoning his, Miranda looked back at the angry wound on Shadow Walker's arm. Fumbling with the medicine pouch, she repeated, "We should've tended to this sooner."

We.

Dipping her finger in the salve, Miranda then smoothed it onto the cut, and Shadow Walker felt the knot deep inside him tighten further. Her stroke was tentative . . . gentle. It touched his heart.

Looking up when she was finished, Miranda attempted a smile, then continued with her last thought as if it had not been broken, "But if this medicine works as well on your arm as it did on my feet, it'll heal in no time."

Her gaze lingered. Hardly aware of her intent, she whispered, "Thank you for saving me from Spotted Bear, Shadow Walker."

Shadow Walker whispered, "Spotted Bear risked his life the moment he said your name. I keep what is mine— and you are mine, Miranda."

Sensing a depth to Shadow Walker's words that went unexpressed, Miranda felt a trembling begin inside her. She remained silent as he continued, "You asked many times where I am taking you. I did not answer when we started our journey because I felt no need—and then because my response became uncertain. But I will tell you our destination now. We go to a place of peace and beauty that I would share with you. At first I saw it as a place of resolution where the battle of wills between us would be settled at last, but I see it now as a place of promise, where we might cast the disputes between our people from our minds—where we might come to know each other without conflict."

Pausing, his voice dropping to a husky whisper, Shadow Walker continued, "But with my answer comes a question that I would not ask before."

Shadow Walker's gaze held hers intently. Miranda felt its warmth caress her, and she felt the honesty it demanded from her in return as he said, "I would share this place with you in harmony, Miranda. Will you travel there with me as a captive, or will you seek a peace between us willingly?"

The glowing warmth in Shadow Walker's gaze enveloped her. Its silent promise touched her heart in a way that left only one response that she could truthfully give.

Miranda whispered, ". . . Willingly."

CHAPTER ELEVEN

Gray streaks of dawn filtered through Major Thurston's office window where he had been waiting, fully dressed and ready to begin his journey, for hours. Too much time had passed since Miranda had disappeared leaving behind only an abandoned hat and a few hoof-prints in the sand. Washington's orders for no aggressive action against the hostiles had rendered the fort's daily patrols pointless, and all other efforts to locate Miranda had failed. Having exhausted all other avenues of appeal, the major had finally realized that a request for an inter-view in Washington was his only hope of effecting a change in policy that might bring Miranda home. He had received permission for the interview by wire the previous day. Weighing heavily on his mind was the possibility that Miranda's life depended on its outcome.

"Your escort is ready, sir."

Frowning, Major Thurston turned toward Lieutenant Hill where the lieutenant awaited a response. He didn't like leaving the fort under Hill's command, even temporarily. Hill had revealed an increasing irrationality with regard to the Indian problem in recent weeks. His uncertainty whether Hill would act on it during his absence was his greatest concern in leaving.

That thought in mind, Major Thurston responded to Hill's poorly concealed impatience. "The escort can wait a few minutes. I have something to say to you first."

The almost imperceptible tightening of Hill's lips did not escape the major's notice when he said, "I'm leaving the fort under your temporary command while I travel to Washington, Lieutenant. I will return as soon as my mission in Washington is accomplished. I want to remind you that General Morton's order still stands. No aggressive action is to be initiated from this fort that will cause any conflict with the hostiles, most especially with the Cheyenne."

His gaze pinning Hill, Major Thurston asked, "Is that understood?"

"Yes, sir."

The major eyed Hill a moment longer. Hill's face flushed an unnatural shade as the major then pressed, "You're a well-trained officer. You know what your orders are. I expect you to follow them."

Approaching to stand a hair's-breadth from Hill's face, Major Thurston continued more softly, "Off the record— I want you to know I'm aware that you consider my efforts on my daughter's behalf ineffective and lacking in courage. I also know you haven't hesitated to voice those opinions to others in the fort. Speaking as a man, I couldn't care less what you think of me as long as you follow my orders . . . but speaking as a father, I want to make perfectly clear that if you use the temporary command of this fort to do anything that will put my daughter's safety in jeopardy—*you're a dead man*. Is that also understood, Lieutenant?"

"Yes, sir."

That message conveyed, Charles strode out of his office toward the escort awaiting him.

The morning dew left a silver sheen on the grass through which Miranda walked as she made her way to the spring. Glancing back, she saw the dark green trail her footsteps had left behind, the only marks to mar the beauty of the meadow that stretched out on all sides of her. She looked up at the snow-topped mountains in the distance that days of journeying had never seemed to bring any closer, and watched as the glow of the new day's sun rose up the slopes with breathtaking beauty.

A cool morning breeze caressed her skin and Miranda smiled. Shadow Walker had brought her to this spot two days earlier, explaining to her that it was a magical place where game was abundant and the days passed untouched, unaltered by the conflicts of the present.

Since they'd arrived, an easy pattern had been established between Shadow Walker and her. Shadow Walker had spent the mornings hunting while she worked around the camp, and during long afternoons they had eaten,

swum, talked, and laughed. As evening shadows lengthened, their confidences had deepened, with Shadow
Walker speaking of his youth with both sadness and joy,
and of his hopes for times to come.

Miranda had not been so candid. Discomfort nudged
at the knowledge that while she had spoken at length
about her earlier life, she had avoided any references to her
father's military status and rank, and the fact that he had
often led his command against the Cheyenne. She had told
herself that the intimacy of those moments was precious
and too tenuous to risk—that she needed more time—but
the passing hours only increased her difficulty.

Making her way toward the pool that glistened in the
rising sun, Miranda glanced only briefly toward the knoll
where her mount grazed protected from clear view. She
knew that leaving the animal behind while he hunted was
another sign of Shadow Walker's trust, and her discomfort
deepened.

Miranda paused at the pool's edge, a recurring guilt
plaguing her. What was her father doing now? Was he suffering because of her? She wished she could talk to him so
she could apologize for her stubbornness in leaving the
fort that day and tell him she loved him. She also wanted to
tell him she had learned a lot since the day of her capture—
about the Cheyenne way of life, the honor they accorded a
battle that was well and honestly waged, and the value they
placed on a person's given word. Most especially, however,

she wanted to tell her father she knew now that Shadow Walker wasn't the savage everyone believed him to be, that he was just a man like any other.

Shadow Walker's image flashed before Miranda, and her heart skipped a beat. No, that was untrue. Shadow Walker was unlike any man she'd ever known.

A frown grew on Miranda's face as another thought nagged. But she couldn't tell her father all those things, because despite the beauty of the past few days, she was still a captive. Shadow Walker and she would eventually return to the Cheyenne camp, and when they did—she could not be certain how it would all end.

Suddenly unwilling to follow those thoughts any further, Miranda walked into the pond. The morning sun was bright on her head as the water soaked through her shirt to cool her skin. Closing her eyes, she forced away her concerns and floated motionlessly on the placid surface.

So absorbed was she that she did not hear the footsteps at the water's edge.

Shadow Walker swam underwater with long, powerful strokes. So relaxed was Miranda while floating on the surface of the pond that she had not heard him return from the hunt. Nor had she seen him turn his mount loose in the knoll before stripping down to his breechcloth to enter the water.

Reaching her side, Shadow Walker broke suddenly

through the surface to Miranda's startled gasp. Momentarily silent, he stared into Miranda's face. Her great, clear eyes were wide with surprise. Heavy droplets of water clung to dark lashes that emphasized their startlingly light color. As he watched, the sun-kissed color of her fair cheeks flushed a darker shade that signaled pleasure at his return—pleasure that raised similar emotions in his own heart. A welcoming smile broke across her lips and he remembered a time when he had wondered with a sinking heart if that smile would ever shine for him.

Breaking the silence between them, Miranda said, "You surprised me. I didn't hear you come back."

Shadow Walker's smile dimmed at Miranda's comment. He replied, "In that lies the danger."

"Danger?" Miranda frowned and glanced around them. "What danger could threaten us in this beautiful place?"

Innocence.

Smiling again, Shadow Walker returned, "There is no danger while I am at your side, Miranda."

Emerging from the pond refreshed a short time later, Shadow Walker sat in the brilliant sunshine at the pool's edge. He smiled as Miranda sat down beside him. He watched as she wrung out her unbound hair, unconsciously separating the strands with her fingers as she said abruptly, "What did you mean when you said there was danger here?"

Shadow Walker did not respond.

"You didn't mean from animals, did you?"

"No."

"Tell me."

Shadow Walker responded evasively, "Caution is prudent wherever we are."

Miranda was confused. She had noted his concern when she failed to hear his return, but she sensed a deeper anxiety than the one he had voiced. She wanted to know what worried him.

But Shadow Walker resisted, and she pressed again, "Shadow Walker—"

"This place deceives, Miranda. Its beauty lulls the senses into believing that beyond this cool pond and green meadow where the sun shines and the sky is clear, blood is no longer spilled."

"But it's different here."

"Yes, here, close to sacred ground, the beauty remains, but it is fragile and must not be taken for granted."

"We're safe here, aren't we?"

Frowning, Shadow Walker replied, "I wish to speak of this no more, for to do so would be to compromise the short time here that remains."

The short time that remains.

Shadow Walker stood up abruptly and Miranda noted again the small scar that marred the smooth expanse of his back. Standing beside him, she touched it tentatively, turning him toward her.

Unwilling to be put off by the darkening of his frown, Miranda said, "I thought you said the Cheyenne wear their scars proudly."

"I do not wish to be reminded of that scar in this place."

"Why?"

"Miranda—"

"I want to know, Shadow Walker."

His dark eyes holding hers with sudden heat, Shadow Walker rasped, "I wear this scar proudly because it reminds me of the bullet a white horse soldier fired into the back of a Cheyenne boy who sought to escape an attack on his unprotected village in the middle of the night. I wear it proudly because that boy survived when most did not; and because the bullet removed from that grievous wound—cast into the fire by the shaman who breathed life back into the boy—signified a burning vengeance to be forever *mine*."

Shadow Walker paused, then continued, "I have wrought that vengeance many times, Miranda, and I will wreak it many more."

"But you said—"

"I said that in this place there is peace. But it is unsafe to assume that we cannot be touched by the outside world here."

As if confirming Shadow Walker's words, the rumble of approaching hooves sounded in the distance. Miranda turned toward the sound with surprise. She squinted to identify the approaching figures, then gasped with incredulity as an army patrol rode into view.

The sight of the familiar blue uniforms raised Miranda's arm toward them in an exultant rush. Stunned when Shadow Walker snatched her down to the ground with his hand covering her mouth, then held her motionless with the weight of his body, she heard him whisper fiercely, "Hear what I say, Miranda, for I tell you now—there is only one way the soldiers will take you from me."

Shadow Walker's words froze Miranda's mind. Somehow unable to think past the inconceivability of the moment, she watched as the patrol drew nearer, then passed so close that she could see Lieutenant Hill's rigid expression, Will Blake's boyish frown, and Sergeant Wallace's invariable scowl. The hilts of their Army sabers glinted in the brilliant sun. Their sheathed rifles bounced against their mounts' sides—and Miranda closed her eyes.

The hoofbeats faded into the distance and Miranda opened her eyes again to see that the patrol had faded from view as well.

Releasing her abruptly, Shadow Walker stood up. His expression unreadable, he towered over her for long, silent moments before he said, "Ready yourself. It is time to leave."

Rattling Blanket's lodge was silent except for the hoarse rasp of her breathing. Beside her sleeping bench,

Walking Bird stood in quiet sorrow. Near the doorway, Two Moons stood similarly composed, her eyes following the actions of the shaman who chanted an ongoing prayer. Engrossed, none looked up at Spotted Bear when he stepped into the doorway and scrutinized the scene with a slitted gaze.

Pausing there, Spotted Bear looked at the old woman lying on the sleeping bench. Her eyes were closed and her breathing was ragged. He had arrived back at the camp to the news that Rattling Blanket had fallen and that she had lapsed into a sleep from which it was feared she would not awaken.

Spotted Bear's chest began a slow heaving. The old witch! She had turned her back on him and walked away when he had attempted to buy the girl from her—but what had stung him most had been the pity in her gaze when she had looked at him.

Pity!

It was all Spotted Bear could do not to laugh aloud. Who was to be pitied now? Surely not he, a Cheyenne warrior with the best of his years before him, while she—a useless, nearly crippled old squaw—lay breathing her last.

Shadow Walker's image rose abruptly before him, and Spotted Bear grunted aloud. The old woman had been Shadow Walker's staunchest defender and his closest link to the past. Her death would be a heavy blow.

Sobering, Spotted Bear turned his back on Rattling

Blanket's lodge and walked away, determined that that blow would be the first of many.

Darkness was descending as Shadow Walker drew his mount to a halt and signaled Miranda to do the same. They had packed up their camp, ending their idyll with haste. They had traveled rapidly, speaking little and halting only to refresh the horses at extended intervals.

Miranda watched as Shadow Walker dismounted, then strode toward her and swung her down from her mount. She noted the caution with which he scrutinized the area, then made preparations for their camp. Halting her when she attempted to gather wood for their fire, he shook his head and said, "We will make no fire tonight."

"But the soldiers are gone. They've probably returned to the fort for the night."

"No campfire."

Miranda unconsciously sighed.

"The soldiers came too close today, Miranda." Shadow Walker's explanation was strained. "We return to camp, where there is greater safety in numbers."

"Back to the camp, where I'm a captive."

Pausing in response, Shadow Walker replied in a gentler tone, "Yes, you are my captive."

"I don't want to go back there, Shadow Walker."

"We will speak no more of this tonight."

Insistent, Miranda replied, "Nothing will change

overnight. I still won't want to go back to the camp tomorrow."

"Miranda," Shadow Walker's words came slowly. "Do you trust that I will protect you in this wilderness?"

Miranda nodded.

"Do you doubt that I would protect you in the same way in the camp that is my home?"

Miranda hesitated.

"Miranda . . ."

She did not reply.

His gaze intent, promise in his voice, Shadow Walker whispered, "You will return with me to the camp. You will be under my protection there, as you have always been, and I will win your trust."

"But—"

"Put aside your protests, Miranda." Sliding his arm around her, Shadow Walker whispered, "Believe in me, so we might not spend this time together in conflict."

Shadow Walker's arm was strong. His words were heavy with promise. They touched her heart—and somehow, Miranda believed.

CHAPTER TWELVE

"You heard me, Sergeant!" Lieutenant Hill's narrow face drew into tight, angry lines as he continued harshly, "I don't care what the news is from Fort Larned. Fort Walters will not enter into military conflict with the Cheyenne unless directly ordered or provoked."

Ignoring Sergeant Wallace's barely concealed sneer, Hill held his temper under tight control. Wallace had boldly entered his office minutes earlier, totally at ease with his insolence in criticizing the temporary command of the fort. Were the situation different and his command permanent, he would not have hesitated to order the burly ignoramus taken into custody and thrown into the guardhouse, where the dolt would remain until his lesson was learned—but his command was not permanent, and he could not afford to alienate totally an aggressive veteran of the Indian wars in whom he might find a handy ally.

Responding to Hill's statement with true arrogance, Wallace replied, "This ain't the way you was talking before Major Thurston left you in charge. Them Cheyenne are raiding all over the frontier while we stay here, sitting on our hands."

"The attacks are localized, initiated by war parties operating apart from the main body of Cheyenne."

"That don't make their victims any less dead."

"Orders come straight from Washington. I can't ignore them."

"Washington ain't here now. Washington don't see them savages burning and looting—"

"As long as Washington's orders hold, I'm bound to obey."

"But—"

"I've answered your concern as best I can, Sergeant, and I don't intend to discuss the matter any further."

"Lieutenant, the men ain't happy about the way things are going. They—"

"This discussion is over."

"The men are saying—"

"You're dismissed, Sergeant!"

His mouth snapping shut, Sergeant Wallace turned with a stiff salute and left the room.

Seething, Lieutenant Hill stared at the door that had closed behind Wallace. He then glanced around Thurston's office, where he had assumed temporary residence, and muttered a curse.

Damn that Thurston! The bastard had deliberately tied his hands and put him in the position where he now looked as cowardly as Thurston had proved himself to be.

Wallace was right. The depredations continued, with Cheyenne war parties raiding with impunity north of the fort. It was just his luck that the sweeping patrols he had personally conducted since Thurston's departure had not netted him direct contact with any hostiles so he might prove his true worth.

Hill's thin lips twitched with suppressed anger. He had personally headed up patrols that had delved deeper into Indian territory than Thurston had ever allowed, hoping for just that opportunity, but fate had cheated him of his quests for glory. The result had been grumbling among the men that appeared to be growing louder with each passing hour—not to mention the direct confrontation with Wallace that he had just terminated.

His agitation overwhelming him, Hill strode to the window and looked out at the fort yard with mounting frustration. He was in command of the fort in name only. Thurston had made a puppet out of him—a creature unworthy to be called a man, much less a soldier!

Trembling with fury, Hill gritted his teeth and vowed: for that humiliation, he would make sure that Thurston paid.

Shadow Walker sat his mount with a warrior's bearing as they approached the Cheyenne camp—a demeanor Miranda had grown to realize was instinctive, born of accomplishment and pride. Miranda kept her gaze straightforward and her chin high in a manner designed to conceal the thundering of her heart and a fear she dared not admit.

Refusing to acknowledge the hostile glances and whispering between the squaws as they entered the camp, Miranda noted that Shadow Walker searched the area with his gaze, his brow furrowing.

Miranda's heart jumped a beat as Walking Woman's broad, familiar figure emerged through the gathering crowd. The squaw called out to Shadow Walker in their native tongue and Shadow Walker reined his mount back abruptly. Uncertain, she listened to the brief exchange between them and saw Shadow Walker react with a sharp nod before nudging his mount again into motion.

Shadow Walker dismounted beside Rattling Blanket's lodge. Miranda followed as he raised the lodge flap and stood hesitantly in the doorway. Behind him, Miranda smelled the scent of burning herbs and heard the shaman's muted chanting. She looked inside the lodge and gasped aloud at the sight of Rattling Blanket lying as still as death on her sleeping bench.

Watching as Shadow Walker entered and kneeled beside the motionless squaw, Miranda felt her throat choke tight. Her actions instinctive, she entered and stood beside him. She saw true anguish in his gaze and felt his grief as Shadow Walker spoke softly to the unconscious woman.

Halting his chanting, Running Elk addressed Shadow

Walker briefly. Shadow Walker stood up, and with a short, backward glance at Rattling Blanket, left the lodge.

Close behind him when he emerged outside, Miranda questioned softly, "What happened? What's wrong with Rattling Blanket?"

Grasping the horses' reins, Shadow Walker turned back toward her, his expression grave. "Rattling Blanket's weak legs failed her as she made her way to the stream, and she fell. She was discovered there long after she had fallen, and her condition has worsened until it is unclear if she will survive."

"Her legs . . ."

Miranda remembered the old squaw's limping gait as she had left the lodge each morning and made her way down the trail for living water—the same water that she had refused to fetch. She recalled that Rattling Blanket's breathing had been labored when returning to the lodge carrying the heavy water sack—the sack she had refused to carry. She also remembered that Rattling Blanket had not rebuked her for her refusal, but instead had shared equally with her. Miranda knew she would not have fared as well with Walking Woman in her rebellion, or with any of the other squaws who looked at her with such contempt.

And she was ashamed.

Miranda felt the distress Shadow Walker restrained as he said, "It was my intention for you to reside with Rattling Blanket until you were able to accept the

Cheyenne way fully. As sister to my mother, Rattling Blanket has always been closer to me than any other squaw. I knew she would care for you well, because she is kind and good, but I know now that cannot be."

Reacting spontaneously, hardly aware of her intent, Miranda responded, "Rattling Blanket can't take care of me as you intended, but I can take care of her."

A trace of a smile touching his lips for the first time that day, Shadow Walker responded, "Were these earlier times, and were you Cheyenne—"

Cutting him short, Miranda replied, "But I'm *not* Cheyenne."

Abruptly solemn, Shadow Walker replied, "You will be."

Noting that she chose neither to accept nor to refute his statement, Shadow Walker continued, "I leave you here as you request, but I will return."

Watching as Shadow Walker turned to lead the horses away, Miranda realized that she was suddenly alone in a place where animosity against her was ever present. She glanced around her, aware that her discussion with Shadow Walker had not gone unwitnessed, then turned back to Rattling Blanket's lodge. Taking a deep breath, she walked inside.

Indian agent Tom Edwards looked at the remains of the burned-out conestoga wagon lying beside the wilderness trail—the result of the latest Indian attack. He studied the area more closely, then turned back toward the Fort

Larned patrol behind him. Nodding, he said, "It was the Cheyenne, all right."

The responsive grumbling of the men was an indication of the heightening heat of the conflict on the frontier, and Edwards frowned. The situation had steadily worsened from the day that Red Shirt had been incarcerated. He couldn't be certain the Thurston girl's capture was directly related to it, but what he was sure of was that Washington had handled both those circumstances poorly. Worse, by refusing to consider all alternate solutions proposed, Washington continued to contribute to a situation which was rapidly reaching catastrophic proportions.

Turning, Edwards scrutinized the faces of the soldiers behind him. The occupants of the wagon had miraculously escaped with their lives, but the men were nonetheless ready to fight at the drop of a hat. He knew how dangerous that was. He needed to defuse the situation—for the sake of the Indians who were his charges and who had no chance at all for ultimate victory, and for the sake of the young men in uniform protecting the frontier.

Mounting, Edwards turned his horse back toward the fort without waiting for the command to follow. He did not pause to make a formal report when he reined up in the fort yard later, but went directly to the telegraph office. There, knowing the time had come for a radical step, he picked up pencil and paper and started to write.

CHAPTER THIRTEEN

The scent of burning herbs was beginning to nauseate Miranda. The din of Running Elk's chant throbbed into her brain.

Dipping a cloth into a bowl nearby, Miranda ran it across Rattling Blanket's lips, but there was no reaction to her ministrations.

Looking up as Running Elk spoke to her in Cheyenne, then turned toward the door, Miranda realized that the elderly shaman had finished his chants for the day. Likewise, Walking Woman had left the lodge a short time earlier—having watched her tend to Rattling Blanket with obvious suspicion through the long hours since she and Shadow Walker had arrived back at the camp earlier that day. Strangely, she hadn't felt annoyed by Walking Woman's suspicion. Instead, she had accepted the fact that she'd done nothing to earn the squaw's trust.

Dipping the cloth back into the bowl, Miranda realized that the water she had used to cool Rattling Blanket's brow had warmed to an undesirable degree. She reached for the water pouch, and silently groaned when she found it empty. Knowing she had no recourse, Miranda picked up the pouch and turned to the door. With a last backward glance toward Rattling Blanket, Miranda started toward the path to the stream.

Miranda walked rapidly, her gaze held straight ahead. She did her best to ignore the comments of the squaws she passed. Unable to understand their language, she had no trouble in recognizing their tone. Animosity sounded the same in any language.

With sudden, bitter amusement, Miranda reminded herself that in this camp, she really had no rights at all— that she was no less a captive at present than she had been that first day when Shadow Walker had delivered her, bound hand and foot and draped over his horse like so much baggage.

Miranda turned down on to the trail to the stream, grateful to escape at last the hostile gazes following her. She made her way cautiously as shadows darkened the pathway. Her stomach rumbled, and she realized for the first time that she was hungry. She'd had nothing to eat since she had arrived at the camp. She was hungry, thirsty, and tired from her exhausting efforts to comfort an old squaw who seemed beyond anyone's help.

But most of all, she missed Shadow Walker.

Where was he? He had been absent from Rattling Blanket's lodge the entire afternoon. She needed to see him, if only to settle the nagging uncertainties that seemed to expand with the shadows.

At the sound of a step behind her, Miranda turned, her expectant smile bright.

Miranda's smile disappeared and her stance went rigid.

Held in dark relief against the brilliant colors of the setting sun, Spotted Bear stood behind her on the trail. She strained to read his expression, but the shadows concealed it. Yet his intent could not be mistaken when he said, "You expected never to see me again, but you were wrong. You feel safe here under Shadow Walker's protection, but you are wrong again."

Struggling against an inner trembling, Miranda asked, "What do you want, Spotted Bear?"

"I want what is rightfully mine."

"What has that to do with me?"

"You are *my* captive—stolen from me by Shadow Walker's trickery."

"That's a lie! It was Shadow Walker who chased me down and captured me, not you. And it was Shadow Walker who brought me back here as his captive."

"That is what you choose to believe."

"You told Shadow Walker that you gave up your claim when he spared your life. Was that a lie, too?"

"It was a convenience that freed me for a greater contest to come."

"I thought the word of a Cheyenne warrior was true."

"I am true to my word when I say that Shadow Walker will not enjoy your comforts much longer."

Incensed, Miranda spat, "You speak bravely when Shadow Walker isn't here to hear you."

"I come to tell you that your efforts are wasted in trying to turn the camp to your favor. All here know who the true enemy is. Unlike Shadow Walker, they will not be deceived by your duplicity in pretending to care for the old woman."

"My duplicity?" Miranda seethed, "If I'm so distrusted here, then perhaps you can convince the camp I should be returned to my people."

"Rather, I would convince the camp to 'honor' you as the white horse soldiers 'honor' Red Shirt."

Attempting to counteract the color she felt drain from her face, Miranda replied, "You don't frighten me. Shadow Walker will—"

Grasping her arms roughly, Spotted Bear pulled Miranda close enough to see the true fierceness of his expression for the first time as he rasped, "*Shadow Walker?* I tire of hearing his name, and I will see the day soon when you will curse his name as well!"

Jerking her arms free, Miranda grated, "Get away from me or I'll call Shadow Walker right now."

"You will not call, for to call would chance that my blade will draw Shadow Walker's blood again—this time more deeply. But I leave you now, because the time is not yet right." Pausing, Spotted Bear grasped a lock of her light hair, then added, "It is not ended between us."

Spotted Bear disappeared from the trail as abruptly as

he had come, leaving Miranda shaken.

Reaching the stream moments later, Miranda submerged the water pouch and waited for it to fill, her mind racing. She couldn't tell Shadow Walker that Spotted Bear had approached her. Spotted Bear was tall and well muscled, a physical match for Shadow Walker in many ways. The combat between them had tested both their strength, and she knew that had the situation been reversed, Spotted Bear would not have hesitated to drive his blade home.

The thought of losing Shadow Walker suddenly more devastating than she could bear, Miranda felt her throat choke tight. She needed to see him, to look up into his eyes and feel his warmth encompass her. She needed to reassure herself that she would not be separated from him.

The water pouch filled, Miranda stood and hurried back up the trail.

Shadow Walker emerged from White Horse's lodge, his body stiff and his mind racing. His idyll with Miranda had taken him away from the camp only briefly, but so much had happened while he was gone. Unable to reach agreement on the offer extended for a peace parley or for a manner in which to free Red Shirt, Standing Elk, Crying Crow, and Buffalo Chaser had spent their frustration by leading raids on the outlying frontier. Angry, White Horse had called them into council. The dispute between them continued.

Shadow Walker had been drawn into a fray that had grown more wrathful with each afternoon hour that had passed. The result was indecision and a mounting vexation at Red Shirt's entrapment that Shadow Walker knew would spawn more violence if a plan of action was not agreed upon soon.

Glancing up at the colors the setting sun had painted against the sky, Shadow Walker frowned. Yet other thoughts presently took precedence in his mind: Rattling Blanket, who lay close to death; and Miranda, whose trust in him was new and fragile.

Kneeling beside Rattling Blanket's sleeping bench minutes later, Shadow Walker looked down into the old squaw's face. Informed by Walking Bird as he approached the lodge that Miranda had been seen carrying an empty water sack toward the stream, he had not been disturbed to find her absent. Instead, deep emotions firmly restrained, he had settled himself beside Rattling Blanket, remembering himself as a child. The gentle squaw had nursed his wounds and had sat with him until the memory of gunfire in the darkness, army bugles, raging flames, and the cries of the dying faded from his ears. He recalled that she had shared Red Shirt's pride in him as he had grown, and that she had looked on him as the son who had been denied her.

Tentatively touching her ragged gray braids, Shadow Walker spoke to Rattling Blanket softly. There was no response. His throat tight, he drew himself slowly to his feet at the sound of familiar footsteps entering the lodge and turned to face Miranda. Noting her expression was shaken, Shadow Walker slipped his arm around her and drew her into the twilight shadows outside the lodge.

The first to break the silence between them, Shadow Walker said in a voice still gruff with emotion, "Running Elk has chanted his prayers and sung his songs to Rattling Blanket's spirit, to no avail. Her spirit lies between two worlds, uncertain which way to turn. We must wait while she finds the path that was meant for her."

Studying Miranda's pale face, Shadow Walker saw sadness there, and an anxiety that caused him concern. He questioned, "Is something wrong, Miranda? Do you fear staying here with Rattling Blanket through the night?"

"No."

"Do you fear for your safety in the camp?"

Miranda's lips twitched in an attempt at a smile. "I'm as safe as I've ever been here."

Shadow Walker studied her more closely. Miranda's great eyes held his. They clung with uncertainty in a way he did not fully comprehend, leaving him unsettled. Reacting instinctively, he slipped his arms around her and drew her against his chest, but the gesture meant to comfort rapidly became more. Miranda's slender form was sweet against him. It raised a tenderness and yearning that touched him in a way he had not been touched before.

Drawing back from Miranda with regret, Shadow

Walker acknowledged those feelings, saying, "The recent journey we undertook was meant to teach a lesson to you, but it taught me as well. To hold you close is balm to my aching spirit. Were these simpler times and were you Cheyenne, I would show my regard for you by waiting for you outside your lodge, where I would enclose you in my robe when you emerged. Heart to heart, thus hidden while in full view of all, we would open our hearts to each other, and an ease between us would grow that would bind us even closer. I would show you honor by bringing gifts to your relatives, and I would wait for the time when you would look on me with favor."

Holding her gaze intently, Shadow Walker continued, "But these are not simpler times, and you are not Cheyenne. You are my captive, yet my feelings for you are no less true. So I tell you now, you need fear nothing while I am near, Miranda. I will protect you with my life, for you have become a part of me. This time between us has become more difficult, but we will—"

The sound of approaching footsteps halted Shadow Walker's words. He turned to see Walking Woman stop a few feet away. Her disapproval apparent, she silently offered two steaming bowls of food. When Shadow Walker had accepted them, she left without speaking a word.

Looking back at Miranda, Shadow Walker felt her confusion, yet he could not suppress a smile when he said,

"All else waits when hunger calls. Come, we will eat."

Miranda took the bowl Shadow Walker offered her and followed him inside the lodge. Unusually silent, she sat beside him on the sleeping bench while they ate.

CHAPTER FOURTEEN

Still seated in the waiting room where he had spent most of the day, Major Thurston looked at the empty chairs around him. The room had previously been filled to capacity. He had waited as those chairs emptied one by one, just as he had during the previous days he had spent in the nation's capital.

Major Thurston remembered his eagerness when his train drew into the station three days earlier. Barely waiting until it shuddered to a halt, he had snatched his bag from the overhead rack. Within the hour he had been seated in the same chair where he sat now.

His thoughts drifting, Charles saw a great wilderness of endless grassland undulating in the breeze. He saw the ragged outlines of rocky buttes jutting awkwardly toward the sky; the sun shining on snow-covered mountain peaks that appeared to blend with the clouds; and faint outlines of dark hills that were a mere whisper in a stillness that was so bright and clear that it questioned belief.

And he saw something else as well.

He saw a flaxen-haired girl riding wildly across the open grassland, laughter on her lips and happiness in her heart as she called back to him, flaunting the exuberance of youth. He felt again his pride and true sense of wonder at the beautiful young woman Miranda had become.

A crushing sense of loss returned. Would he ever see Miranda again?

Suddenly despising himself for his momentary doubt, Major Thurston turned his attention to the bespectacled clerk seated at the desk near the office door—the same fellow who had called out names that had gradually emptied all the waiting room chairs but his.

Major Thurston withdrew his watch from his pocket. One glance confirmed that it would not be long before the clerk would start stacking his work on his desk to leave.

His jaw tight with frustration, the major stood up and approached the clerk's desk. He was about to speak when a bell in the interior office turned the clerk up to him to say, "The Secretary will see you now, Major."

Walking through the doorway marked Secretary of the Interior moments later, Major Thurston accepted the Secretary's hand when it was offered to him in greeting. He saw the telegram the Secretary held as he said, "I've received a wire from the frontier. The situation there is deteriorating badly. It looks like we have a lot to discuss."

Miranda awakened with a start. Momentarily disoriented as dawn filtered through the smoke outlet of

Rattling Blanket's lodge, she glanced around her. She took a moment to gather her thoughts, then remembered that since returning to the camp with Shadow Walker days earlier, she had spent her time tending to the injured Rattling Blanket, who had not yet awakened from her unnatural sleep.

With chilling discomfort, Miranda recalled Spotted Bear approaching her with open threats when she went to the stream for living water the first day. For fear of another confrontation between the two braves, she had kept Spotted Bear's threats secret from Shadow Walker—another secret she kept uneasily.

She remembered that Shadow Walker had visited often during the days past, and that the squaws looked at her with open animosity and speculative glances when she was unable to conceal her pleasure in Shadow Walker's company.

Soberly, Miranda remembered something else. During the silence of the night most recently past, she had been driven to speak to Rattling Blanket, even though she had known the words would go unheard when she had whispered, "I'm sorry, Rattling Blanket. Pride and fear kept me from acknowledging—even to myself—the many kindnesses you showed me when I was first brought to this camp. But I want you to know now that I appreciated them, more than you will ever know."

A sense of uneasiness gradually drew Miranda from her wandering thoughts. Something she could not quite define was different in the lodge. A scent . . . a sound . . .

Miranda gasped in sudden realization. Rattling Blanket's labored breathing—it had stopped!

Jumping to her feet on shaky legs, Miranda rushed to Rattling Blanket's sleeping bench and kneeled beside it. The old squaw was so still. Reaching out tentatively, she touched Rattling Blanket's cheek, then gulped in stunned disbelief when the old squaw opened her eyes.

Hardly daring to believe her ears, Miranda heard Rattling Blanket rasp, "I thirst."

Grasping the cup nearby, Miranda poured water into it and held it to Rattling Blanket's lips. Trembling, she watched the old woman swallow awkwardly, then nod her appreciation before closing her eyes.

Waiting only to be certain Rattling Blanket's breathing was normal and steady, Miranda threw open the door flap and raced through the rapidly lightening camp toward Shadow Walker's lodge. Reaching it, she ignored the disapproving glances sent her way and called out in a shaky voice, "Shadow Walker, are you in there?"

Straight from his sleeping bench, his chest and feet bare, Shadow Walker was beside her in a moment. Looking up at him with a sudden sob, Miranda gasped, "Rattling Blanket woke up!"

Shadow Walker kneeled beside Rattling Blanket's sleeping bench, his emotions barely contained. He had slept poorly through the night as his mind had moved in dizzying circles: Red Shirt, still confined; factions of the camp in deep dispute; Rattling Blanket near death; and Miranda. He had finally fallen asleep, only to be awakened by Miranda's excited call.

Incredulous, Shadow Walker looked down at Rattling Blanket. The gentle squaw had opened her eyes as if sensing his presence the moment he entered the lodge.

Grasping her callused hand, Shadow Walker held it tightly as he whispered, "You have been drifting in a netherworld for many days. It was feared you would not return to us."

Her voice a bare rasp of sound, Rattling Blanket replied, "I heard your voices and I could not stay away."

Beside him, Miranda poured water into a cup and held it to Rattling Blanket's lips. The old squaw drank, her eyes briefly brightening as she said, "Dancing Star's spirit returns."

His own throat tight, Shadow Walker turned at that moment to see Running Elk stand briefly in the doorway before entering the lodge. When he looked back at Rattling Blanket, she had lapsed again into a normal sleep.

Yielding his place at Rattling Blanket's side to the aged shaman, Shadow Walker drew Miranda outside. He saw that she was trembling, and that her great, light eyes were moist. But he saw something else as well.

Dancing Star's spirit returns.

Yes, he saw what Rattling Blanket saw. Dancing Star had been named for her spirit and zest for life. He realized he had recognized those same qualities in Miranda the first time he saw her smile.

And she was his.

His heart suddenly pounding, Shadow Walker slipped his arms around Miranda and lowered his mouth to hers. His kiss lingering, he tasted the sweetness of the lips she offered him freely, and the love he had held at bay surged deep and true.

Uncaring of watchful eyes, knowing the time would never be more right, Shadow Walker drew Miranda closer.

He flaunted her!

Rigid with jealousy, Spotted Bear stood a distance away as Shadow Walker embraced the girl. He saw Shadow Walker draw her tight against his chest, melding her to him. He saw the girl's arms slip around his neck to clutch him tight in return. He watched as Shadow Walker's fingers wound in the girl's light hair, as Shadow Walker whispered in her ear and the girl drew back to look up expectantly into his eyes.

Was the girl's power over Shadow Walker so great that he could not see her as she truly was—that she lied, just as all her people lied? Did Shadow Walker not realize the girl waited for the moment when he would be at his weakest so she might use him for her designs?

Fool!

Spotted Bear's lips tightened into a hard line. The girl would not use *him*. Rather, when the girl was his, it would be he who wielded the power and proved who was master.

Running Elk emerged unexpectedly from Rattling Blanket's lodge, his lined face unreadable. Glancing briefly at Shadow Walker and the girl, the old man then strode toward Walking Woman's lodge and went inside.

Satisfaction settled within Spotted Bear as Running Elk disappeared inside Walking Woman's lodge. Running Elk had been witness to Shadow Walker's fascination with the girl. Shadow Walker's image had already begun to tarnish. It would not be long now.

CHAPTER FIFTEEN

The small, hard body hit Miranda full force—with a giggle. Startled, Miranda steadied herself as she looked up from her position beside the stream where she had earlier joined the squaws to wash clothes. A two-year-old stared back at her, his dark eyes sparkling with mischief as he grasped a lock of her hair and yanked it hard.

"Ouch!"

Unable to hold back a smile when the child laughed aloud at her surprised exclamation, Miranda took the chubby hand still holding her hair and extended the lock full length, saying, "You can't have it. It's attached to my head."

Surprising her, the child threw his arms around her neck and held her tight while he pushed his face into her hair and breathed deeply. Unable to resist, Miranda returned the boy's embrace with a quick hug. She drew back when a sober-faced squaw appeared beside them and took the protesting child away with a few words in Cheyenne that somehow lacked the former animosity against her.

Sighing as the child was restored to his mother's side,

Miranda turned back to her laundry. She brushed a spot of water from the simple doeskin garment she now wore, remembering the moment when Rattling Blanket—now recuperated from her accident three weeks earlier—gave her the doeskin dress and a pair of carefully beaded moccasins to wear. She remembered the old squaw's eyes had been moist, and that she had beamed with pride when Miranda emerged from the lodge wearing them minutes later. Miranda had not needed to be told that the dress and moccasins had formerly belonged to Dancing Star, and that Rattling Blanket had given them to her with true affection.

Sighing again, Miranda knew that although some things had changed during the weeks she had been in the camp, others had not. The controversy over Red Shirt's confinement had resulted in the Cheyennes' refusal to attend the peace talks that Washington had proposed, and tensions continued to abound. Her personal duties had eased with Rattling Blanket's recovery, but her position remained unchanged, with no word at all that inquiries about her had even reached the camp.

Glancing around her as she wrung out her shirt, Miranda saw the squaws glance in her direction, then whisper among themselves—but with more curiosity than hostility. She remembered her surprise when one of the younger squaws actually smiled at her that morning. She had smiled back, her heart lighter, but the weight had quickly returned, a weight that Miranda knew would not be lifted until Shadow Walker returned from a mysterious mission that had already lasted three days.

Standing, Miranda smoothed her doeskin dress, then picked up her shirt and started up the trail toward an area with low-lying bushes where the squaws normally spread their laundry out to dry. She missed Shadow Walker desperately. She had not realized how dependent she had become on his presence.

Miranda's conscience nagged abruptly. Shadow Walker had talked freely of so many things during the time they had spent together, making the secret she kept about her father's military status more difficult to carry with every passing day. Yet, while conscious of the danger to the Cheyenne camp if her father attempted to rescue her, she was still unable to speak the words that would alert the camp to that possibility and risk her father's life even further.

Deep in her confused thoughts, Miranda gave a startled cry when strong hands reached out from the bordering foliage to snatch her off the trail. She gasped when familiar arms encircled her, then whispered Shadow Walker's name as his mouth met hers. Returning his kiss with spontaneous joy, she slipped her arms around his neck, tangling her hands in the raven-colored hair that hung unbound onto his shoulders as he crushed her close.

Drawing back at last, Shadow Walker devoured Miranda with his gaze before whispering, "The days have been long and the hours slow since I last held you in my arms." Pausing only for a lingering kiss, he continued, "Were these different days, more time would be ours so I could prove my feelings for you."

Accepting Shadow Walker's words, grateful that he had not returned wearing war paint as she had secretly dreaded, Miranda whispered, "If only our people understood each other better, things would be different. Washington is too far removed from the frontier to be able to see the full picture here. All they see is the blood that's been shed."

Shadow Walker did not respond.

Miranda continued spontaneously, "Maybe I could make a difference, Shadow Walker. If you let me return, I could go to Washington and speak for the Cheyenne."

"No."

"I could tell the truth, that the Cheyenne don't trust Washington's word anymore, that the Cheyenne believe if their chiefs went to the parley Washington is proposing, they'd be imprisoned just as Red Shirt was. I could make them understand."

"No!"

"Shadow Walker—"

His hands gripping her shoulders, Shadow Walker rasped, "Speak of this no more."

"Shadow Walker, please—"

Releasing her abruptly, Shadow Walker strode back out onto the trail.

Standing frozen into stillness for long moments, Miranda was stunned by her own unexpected plea. What did she really want? Surely not to be separated from this man who stirred her so deeply.

That thought suddenly unbearable, Miranda raced after Shadow Walker. She reached him as he mounted his horse. Her heart aching when he looked down at her coldly and turned his horse away, she was certain of only one thing—that her heart was breaking.

Shadow Walker hesitated as he prepared to ride off. Miranda had raced to follow him, and she was looking up at him with great, light eyes despairing.

Despite himself, Shadow Walker felt his anger weakening. His scouting mission to Fort Lyon where Crying Crow, Buffalo Chaser, and he had watched the fort for several days, hoping to discover a way to rescue Red Shirt, had met with failure. He had returned and spoken to White Horse, and had then gone directly to seek Miranda—but his joy in seeing her again had been short lived.

Contradictions assailed him: Miranda was beautiful in ways he had not previously considered beautiful, yet her beauty touched him deeply; she was strong in ways that raised his ire, yet those ways demanded his respect; her mind was sharp and quick, occasionally fostering suspicion, yet she spoke with a truth and candor that he could not deny. Staring down at her a moment longer, he acknowledged something else as well—that in spite of those contradictions, Miranda had found a place in his heart that no one could replace.

Reaching down abruptly, Shadow Walker swung Miranda up onto his horse in front of him. His arms tight around her, he drew her back against him, then kicked his mount into a full gallop. Traveling at a furious pace, he did not draw back on the reins until his mount was deeply lathered and the camp had disappeared into the distance behind them.

Miranda made no sound when he turned his horse toward a shady patch nearby, then dismounted and lifted her to the ground. She did not speak as he drew her into a crushing embrace.

Miranda responded to his kiss and he felt the fluttering of her heart against his chest. Drawing back from her, Shadow Walker whispered, "Would you so easily sacrifice this bond between us so you could return to your people?" When she hesitated, he pressed, "Yet you would leave me now if I allowed it?"

"No . . . yes . . . I mean—" Miranda's words were shaken. "I don't know."

Shadow Walker studied Miranda's moist gaze, her trembling lips. Her conflicted emotions touched a chord that melted the hard core of his anger. A new swell of tenderness rising within him, he consoled her in the only way he could when he whispered at last, "Do not concern yourself with an answer, Miranda. I will see to it that you never need to make a choice."

Riding at the head of his escort as the sun reached its apex, Charles approached Fort Walters. He had stepped down from the train and had then boarded an overland stage that had rattled and shaken its way along the rutted trails. He had looked out the window of the coach at the wilderness terrain to see that the driver maintained a relentless pace with a watchful eye, despite the presence of the heavily armed guard seated beside him and the two additional guards riding behind—all silent testimony to the continuing deterioration of the situation on the frontier.

Major Thurston frowned at the thought that ironically, the worsening condition on the frontier had worked out to his advantage in Washington. It had provided the final thrust necessary to gain acceptance of his new proposal, which had been forwarded ahead from Washington to the frontier by wire, with instructions for Indian agent Edwards to offer it immediately to the Cheyenne.

Relieved to be riding through Fort Walters's gates again at last, the major then dismounted and turned toward the contingent awaiting him. Lieutenant Hill stood in front, his expression cold. Standing beside Hill, his round face wreathed in smiles, was Indian agent Edwards.

Stepping forward as Major Thurston dismounted,

Lieutenant Hill offered with sincerity sadly lacking, "Welcome back, Major."

In sharp contrast, Edwards extended his hand with a hearty laugh, saying, "Well, you did it! You finally got Washington to authorize something that might actually make a difference out here. Congratulations!"

Major Thurston's expression was sober as he replied, "Your telegram provided exactly the support I needed to win my case, Edwards. I'm obliged. What I want to hear you say now is that you've already forwarded the proposal on to the Cheyenne."

"I sent it days ago."

Turning back to Lieutenant Hill, Major Thurston ordered, "Dismiss my escort and see that they're fed and given bunks for the night. They'll be returning to Fort Rankin in the morning. You can join Edwards and me in my office when you're finished."

Lieutenant Hill's orders echoed behind him as Major Thurston started toward his office with Edwards. A caustic smile touched the major's lips. From the look of Hill, things hadn't gone the way he had wanted at the fort. That was a shame. He hoped Hill wasn't disenchanted with the glory of command.

Spotted Bear watched as the military contingent he had been awaiting disappeared within the gates of Fort Walters. Turning to the scouting party behind him, he spat a few sharp words, then turned back to his surveillance of the fort. The soldiers believed themselves far above the Cheyenne, but fools that they were, they did not realize their Indian scouts were faithful to the Cheyenne and had warned them that the fort commander would soon return with new orders from Washington.

A contemptuous growl sounded low in Spotted Bear's throat. He was not dismayed. His people were at the end of their patience. Another proposed treaty would be his chance to convince the last dissenters in his tribe that there was only one way to deal with those who spilled Cheyenne blood.

With a quick gesture to his men, Spotted Bear turned and headed back in the direction of camp. He would await the arrival of the communication there, knowing that with the return of Major Thurston, the moment of full glory was nearing.

CHAPTER SIXTEEN

Rattling Blanket limped out of her lodge and looked around her. The sun had passed the midpoint in the clear sky. Its rays were bright and warm on her shoulders, numbing the aches that still remained from her fall weeks earlier.

Her mind slipping back to those dark days, Rattling Blanket recalled the haze of pain and heat in which she had drifted until Shadow Walker's voice stirred her from those shadows and she then heard the girl's whispered words of regret. Her spirit was renewed at that moment, and the echoes of those two voices had guided her back.

A smile touching her lips, Rattling Blanket exalted in her return to health. She was grateful that her mind was now clear, and that during her recovery, with Miranda at her side, she had come to know the golden-haired one's heart. Her faith had been restored.

Her brief smile fading, Rattling Blanket turned again to scan the surrounding area. Miranda had left the lodge earlier. Although concerned that the girl had not yet returned, she did not choose to inquire of the squaws where Miranda might be, aware that although their animosity had softened, they still held themselves apart from her. She knew Spotted Bear was reportedly absent from camp, but she also knew his continuing lust for the girl and jealousy of Shadow Walker had not abated. Uncertain if he had returned, she feared the outcome if Spotted Bear had waylaid her.

Sensing a presence behind her, Rattling Blanket turned abruptly to see Two Moons standing there. She frowned as the old woman observed, "You look for someone whom you fear, and you fear for someone who holds a place in your heart."

Nodding, Rattling Blanket waited. Two Moons had been a silent presence in her lodge during her recovery. She had spoken little to Miranda, choosing instead to visit when Miranda was absent from the lodge. Rattling Blanket knew that Two Moons had not told anyone about her vision out of deference to her, but she sensed a change. Reluctant to hear what the old woman had to say, she did not encourage her to speak, but Two Moons would not be silenced.

Persevering, Two Moons began, "The girl has been absent from your lodge for many hours."

"I am concerned only for her safety."

"The girl gains acceptance in the camp."

"Because she has proved her worthiness."

"Because Running Elk relates to all who will listen that

you were close to death, were deaf to his supplications, and were slowly slipping from his grasp when the girl returned. He speaks of observing from the doorway as you awakened with the girl beside you—and witnessing the moment when Dancing Star's spirit entered the girl's heart to draw you back."

Surprised at Two Moons's revelation, yet sensing a dark moment to come, Rattling Blanket maintained her silence as the old woman continued, "I have attempted to yield to Running Elk's words. I have fought to accept his wisdom, but I can keep silent no longer."

Two Moons's gaze grew intense. "The vision returned last night. I saw our people crying in despair as flames consumed our lodges, as gunfire and long knives slashed the air. Amid it all, I saw the girl seated on her mount with the white man's horse soldiers surrounding her. At her feet, I saw Shadow Walker lying—"

"I will listen no more!"

Anguish visible in the deep lines of her face, Two Moons whispered, "My silence weighs heavily on my heart. I would speak and give fair warning to our people."

"If you speak, the camp will strike Running Elk's words from mind and act against the girl. Shadow Walker will be raised to fury and Cheyenne will draw Cheyenne blood, lending a truth to your vision that you do not desire."

"Blood will be shed. I saw it!"

"You are old. Your sight becomes confused."

"My body ages, but my visions are clear."

Panicking at the old woman's determined response, Rattling Blanket said, "Warn if you must, but speak to Shadow Walker first, for it is he whom your vision concerns."

"Shadow Walker's heart has been touched by the girl. He will not listen."

"Shadow Walker's heart is Cheyenne."

Considering Rattling Blanket's words for a silent moment, Two Moons replied, "You would place the weight of all I have seen on Shadow Walker's shoulders? It is a heavy burden indeed."

"Shadow Walker's shoulders are broad and his strength unfailing. The fate of the Cheyenne will rest safely there."

Her intense gaze lingering a moment longer, Two Moons nodded, then turned away.

His mount spent and lathered from the relentless pace he had traveled since leaving Fort Walters behind, Spotted Bear grunted with satisfaction when the Cheyenne camp finally came into view. He glanced back at the braves behind him and saw that Eagle Feather and Runs With Wolves appeared equally glad that their scouting party was nearing home at last.

Slowing his approach, Spotted Bear sneered. His reasons were not the same as Eagle Feather's, whose thoughts now centered on the skinny squaw waiting for him in his lodge. Nor did he share Runs With Wolves's eagerness to return so he might join the next raiding party to leave the camp. His intentions went deeper than those feeble ambitions. Instead, he looked to a time when he would establish a fame with the Cheyenne that would outrank that of the noblest warrior of his tribe—when he would then make certain that Shadow Walker's legend did not survive because Shadow Walker would not survive.

As if in response to his thoughts, Spotted Bear saw a rider rapidly approaching from the opposite direction. The rider came from the direction of Black Hand's camp— Black Hand, close friend to Indian agent Tom Edwards.

His scrutiny intensifying, Spotted Bear saw the rider slide his mount to a halt at the edge of the camp, then dismount to walk swiftly toward White Horse's lodge.

Spotted Bear recognized the rider to be Leaning Tree, renowned in Black Hand's camp as his swiftest messenger. Suddenly certain that the time had come, that Black Hand's messenger was even now delivering the new offer from Washington, Spotted Bear kicked his exhausted mount forward, so he might be present to guide the future on its way.

"Sir, I wish to make a statement."

Lieutenant Hill struggled to restrain his contempt as Major Thurston turned toward him with a raised brow.

The major had retired to his office with Indian agent Edwards upon his return to Fort Walters a short time earlier. Hill had joined them within minutes, and had listened, silently irate, while the specifics of the offer forwarded to the Cheyenne were enumerated.

Waiting until Thurston signaled him to continue, Hill said, "I feel it is my duty to state for the record that I disagree with the policy being established by your offer to the Cheyenne."

Thurston replied coolly, "What are your objections, Lieutenant?"

Hill replied with growing heat, "I feel the proposal is an abomination, sir."

"An abomination?"

"Instead of making these savages understand that we will never allow them to win a war against us, you are *appealing* to them—making them think that they have rights in this struggle for the frontier."

"They *do* have rights."

"Do they?" Hill gave a scoffing snort. "They won't stop killing and butchering while there's a single one of them left alive, and the sooner the US military realizes that, the better."

"I think you've said enough, Lieutenant."

"Your offer will prolong our fight for sovereignty on the frontier."

"Lieutenant—"

"The blood of every soldier that's shed because of it will be on your hands."

His gaze narrowing, Thurston responded unexpectedly, "You don't fool me, Lieutenant."

His agitation barely restrained, Hill returned, "I don't know what you mean."

"You came to the frontier looking for glory as an Indian fighter, and you didn't find it. Your attitude brought you discredit, and frustration embittered you. You don't care about the blood that might be shed, as long as it isn't your own, and as long as it looks good on your record."

"That's not true."

"Isn't it?" His jaw tight, Thurston continued, "I think it is. I will, however, see to it that your statement goes on the record. With it will go my evaluation, stating that an officer like you has no place on the frontier. That said, I want to make clear that since you are here and in my service, I expect you to disregard your personal opinions to follow orders without exception. Is that understood?"

"Yes, sir."

"I promise you, that when this present crisis is settled, I will do my best to see that you are given an assignment elsewhere, where your personal convictions will not be in such sharp conflict with your duty."

"Yes, sir."

"In light of the circumstances, you won't be needed during this briefing any longer. You are dismissed."

Snapping a sharp salute, Lieutenant Hill turned on his heel, and left the room. Drawing the door closed behind him, he paused in an effort to control his outrage.

. . . I'll do my best to see that you'll be placed on assignment else-where . . .

He knew what that meant. Reassignment accompanied by a negative evaluation—another blot on his record that would end his military career.

Humiliation. Failure!

Hill started stiffly down the hallway.

"Lieutenant."

Turning abruptly toward the familiar voice, Hill saw Sergeant Wallace standing in the shadows a few feet away. When he did not respond, Wallace asked boldly, "What's going on in there? I'm hearing a lot of rumors that don't sound too good to me. You ain't going to stand by and let them two turn things around so's the Cheyenne get away with everything they've done, are you?"

Hill still did not respond and Wallace asked harshly, "Ain't you got nothing to say? What are you going to do about what's happening?"

Hill stared at the burly sergeant.

Yes, what *was* he going to do about it?

Surrounded by warriors convened in council, White Horse addressed Shadow Walker.

"By what name is your captive called by her people?"

Shadow Walker did not immediately respond. He had arrived back at the camp with Miranda only minutes earlier and had been immediately called to White Horse's lodge with the other warriors of his camp. He had been surprised to see Leaning Tree standing beside the chief, and the beating of his heart had quickened at the realization that only a message of great importance would ride with Black Hand's messenger.

Yet White Horse had begun by asking Miranda's name.

At Shadow Walker's hesitation, White Horse held up the sheet in his hand. His heavy features tightly composed, he continued, "This paper comes from the Great White Father in Washington. It speaks of Red Shirt and of a new wisdom that seeks to deal more fairly with the Cheyenne."

His attention acute at the mention of Red Shirt's name, Shadow Walker responded, "How does this 'new wisdom' relate to my captive?"

Still clutching the missive tightly, White Horse continued, "This paper also speaks of a girl believed to have been taken captive by the Cheyenne. This girl is important to the white man's horse soldiers because her father sits high in rank among them. They seek her return. The Great White Father hopes to prove the intentions of his new wisdom with an exchange of captives—Red Shirt for this girl."

"My captive is not the girl you seek." Responding

without hesitation, Shadow Walker continued, "She has spoken of her father, but has never claimed him to be a horse soldier—which she would proudly have done if it were true."

"The daughter of the horse soldier is named Miranda, as it is said within the camp that your captive is also named."

Momentarily taken aback, Shadow Walker insisted, "It is another girl."

"Her father is Major Thurston, who commands at Fort Walters."

Shadow Walker shook his head.

"The girl they seek has yellow hair and her eyes are the color of the sky, similar to your captive."

It could not be.

"She was taken while riding alone on a great black mare, near the ranch of settlers known to the white man by the name *Calhoun*."

But it was.

Shadow Walker went suddenly still. Incredulity claimed his senses. Miranda, the daughter of an important horse soldier—a truth kept carefully concealed from him through long hours while they had talked; a truth that she knew would endanger the camp if her presence there became known to her father; a truth held secret to give clear advantage to the white man's horse soldiers, with no thought to the Cheyenne blood that might be shed should they come to rescue her.

Shadow Walker replied, "Yes, my captive is the girl the soldiers seek."

His scrutiny intense, White Horse continued, "To prove their good will, the horse soldiers would exchange Red Shirt for the girl at a time and place that we would name—the exchange to be followed later by a council to set aside differences, so we might go forward in peace."

"Peace . . ." Miranda's duplicity burning deep, Shadow Walker hissed, "You would trust words of peace when such words have been so easily cast aside before?"

"I would trust if Red Shirt rode free again." His brow furrowed, White Horse turned to scrutinize the warriors who had kept their silence, seeking their reaction.

"Red Shirt for the girl!" Speaking up with sudden zeal, Spotted Bear turned toward Shadow Walker, continuing, "I would accept that exchange gladly to gain Red Shirt's freedom. When Red Shirt walks free again, we may then test more thoroughly the Great White Father's hunger for peace."

An affirmative murmur rose from the warriors assembled and Spotted Bear's gaze glowed with triumph.

Maintaining a stiff silence, Shadow Walker sought to absorb the startling revelations:

Miranda, who had betrayed him with her silence, to be exchanged for Red Shirt.

Red Shirt to be freed without the shedding of blood.

Peace to be discussed with trust and candor evoked by the exchange.

All would come to pass if he agreed to surrender Miranda.

That decision suddenly beyond him, Shadow Walker abruptly strode from the council, leaving a deadening silence behind him. Walking past Miranda when she stepped into his path, he was about to mount his horse when a feeble voice turned him to see Two Moons. The old squaw raised a hand toward him in a silent plea. He stood motionless as she whispered, "I must speak to you before you leave. I must tell you of a vision I saw in the flames. I saw blood. I heard the dying cries of our people. I saw the girl seated among the horse soldiers. She—"

Thrusting Two Moons roughly aside, Spotted Bear interrupted her recitation. He glared at Shadow Walker and spat in a voice carrying clearly within the camp, "Shadow Walker turns his back on the council. The girl has made a woman of him! Rather than surrender her, he would forsake his debt to Red Shirt and allow a great warrior of his people to die in bondage. He dishonors his Cheyenne blood and disgraces his people!"

Then, addressing Shadow Walker directly, his voice deepening with contempt, Spotted Bear added, "I charge Shadow Walker here, in the presence of all, to remember that he is Cheyenne."

Spotted Bear's words rang on the silence as Shadow

Walker scanned the circle gathering around them. He saw warriors by whose sides he had fought and shed blood; and squaws, young and old, widows and young matrons, awaiting his reply. To the rear, White Horse remained silent and intent, while Two Moons looked at him with eyes that were dark pinpoints of light.

Apart from them all stood Miranda, her pale face drained of color.

Shadow Walker held Miranda's gaze. She had betrayed him. With sudden clarity, he realized he had allowed her a victory over him in a way he had never envisioned—that in the intimate battle waged between them, he had somehow allowed their positions to become reversed so that he had become Miranda's captive.

Self-contempt rising full and hot inside him, Shadow Walker addressed White Horse. His voice carrying clearly to the assembled crowd, he said simply, "The girl is yours to do with as you choose."

Ignoring the sound of Miranda's gasp, Shadow Walker mounted up and left the camp behind him.

CHAPTER SEVENTEEN

Major Thurston and a mounted contingent three hundred strong rode with solemn caution through the midmorning sunlight of the wilderness terrain. Aware that his men's sober expressions did not reflect unanimous approval of the endeavor before them, Major Thurston glanced at Tom Edwards, who rode at his side. The silent Indian agent was as somber as they were.

Glancing back at the Indian riding in the center of a heavily armed detail, Major Thurston frowned. The past week had been fraught with tension as the fort waited for a response to the exchange offered to the Cheyenne. The exchange was accepted and agreement had been reached on a neutral location where it was to take place, yet tension had intensified when Red Shirt was delivered to Fort Walters in preparation for the exchange.

Standing tall and proud despite his harsh extended confinement, Red Shirt had not spoken a word upon entering the fort—but the aura of power emanating from the proud warrior had been almost palpable. The men in his command had reacted strongly, necessitating warnings that he knew had chafed.

An hour's eastward travel lay before them, confirming that the sun would be at the Cheyennes' back when they met—a simple advantage that Major Thurston knew was not accidental. Fearful of upsetting the delicate balance of negotiations, he had accepted the location that Chief White Horse had chosen despite his misgivings at the unfamiliarity of the territory. He had countered that deficiency by ordering two patrols to travel at the outskirts of their contingent to scout for suspicious circumstances.

Major Thurston's concerns deepened at the sight of Lieutenant Hill's scowl where he rode at the head of Red Shirt's guard. Unwilling to allow Hill to ride at his side in a position of confidence, he had chosen instead to place Hill where he would retain an *appearance* of confidence—an uncomfortable necessity until he was able to effect the man's transfer.

Turning back toward the trail ahead, Major Thurston concentrated on the exchange to occur and the knowledge that at that very moment, Miranda was traveling toward them—and toward her freedom.

Miranda would soon be safe at home, where she belonged.

That thought foremost, Major Thurston also reminded himself that in saving his daughter, he was also advancing the cause of peace by allowing the military the opportunity for a legitimate exchange that would set to rights a flagrant violation of a truce—a dishonorable act perpetrated against the Cheyenne that never should have occurred.

A legitimate exchange. A step toward peace. Miranda delivered back safely to him.

Major Thurston's concerned scrutiny of the terrain grew more vigilant. Just one more hour.

The rolling grassland stretched out interminably into the distance as Miranda sat her horse in silence. Sober-faced warriors surrounded her where she remained at the rear of the Cheyenne force that had gathered over the past week in preparation for the exchange.

Ahead to her right, Miranda saw Black Hand's warriors sat their horses, prepared for whatever the next few hours would bring. Ahead to her left, she saw White Horse and his braves appeared equally solemn . . . and ready. Miranda's gaze lingered on Shadow Walker, where he sat mounted at White Horse's right, and her throat choked tight. Shadow Walker had attempted no contact with her since the moment when he had renounced his claim on her and walked away.

Miranda forced back the familiar pain that memory evoked. During the long days between, while she had remained in Rattling Blanket's lodge with guards at the door, Spotted Bear's denouncement of Shadow Walker had resounded in her ears. The stinging realization that she was the cause of Shadow Walker's humiliation had tormented her. The long nights had been the hardest, however, while thoughts of Shadow Walker's tenderness, his gentle touch and loving words, had wrung her heart dry.

Feeling the heat of someone's gaze, Miranda turned abruptly to see Spotted Bear staring at her from where he sat mounted a distance from the assembled braves. She saw a hard smile touch his lips, and a chill ran down her spine at its silent menace. Refusing to allow its intimidation, she dismissed him with a glance, then turned back to the terrain ahead.

Her heart beginning a slow pounding, Miranda saw movement in the distance. She stared, refusing to surrender the sight until an advancing military column came clearly into view.

Father.

Suddenly breathless, a tremulous smile on her lips, Miranda struggled to maintain control of her emotions. She had missed him so much. She needed her father to know she was all right. She needed to see him smile. She needed to hear him say he forgave her for the anxiety she had caused him. She needed—

Turning, Miranda saw Shadow Walker looking back at her, his eyes dark with an emotion she dared not name.

Shadow Walker turned away from her abruptly,

and Miranda's thoughts stopped cold. Tears welling, she realized that she had lost him.

And her heart was broken.

The anger seething within Lieutenant Hill came to full, virulent life as the Cheyenne delegation came into view. Turning briefly for a malicious glance at Red Shirt, he then snapped a short command, detached himself from his position, and spurred his mount out of the military column. He rode boldly toward a nearby wooded expanse where he then waited, concealed from view, while his thoughts revolved in heated retrospect.

His career was over—and it wasn't his fault! He had done only what any self-respecting officer in the service of his country would do. He had identified the enemy and had sought to crush it. He would have succeeded, too, if not for a cowardly frontier hierarchy that refused to take necessary action and sought to make him its scapegoat.

Glancing at the mounted column continuing its advance, Hill sneered. A peaceful exchange was a joke that no one appeared to appreciate but him. Why couldn't they all see the truth? Why didn't they realize that as soon as Red Shirt was exchanged for the girl and skirted back to safety, the Cheyenne would attack again, that they'd keep on attacking until the frontier ran red with blood—all while his promising career lay in tatters and he was forced to return home a failure?

Shaking with barely controlled fury, Hill gave a caustic laugh. No, that wouldn't happen. He had already arranged for the inevitable to occur a little earlier than the Cheyenne had planned—and he had made provisions for what would follow.

Seeking out Major Thurston's figure where he rode at the head of the army contingent, Hill muttered, "Fool . . . enjoy your moment. It won't last much longer."

As if in response to that thought, the sound of hoof-beats from the rear turned Hill toward Sergeant Wallace as he reined up beside him. Quizzing the burly sergeant sharply, Hill snapped, "Where's the rest of the scouting patrol? They don't know you came here to meet me, do they?"

"No, sir! I hand-picked Higgins, Blake, Madison, and Carter for the patrol because they're young and green as grass. They were too stupid to suspect anything when I told them to go back to the column while I did a last sweep of the area." Breathless with excitement, Sergeant Wallace continued in a rush, "And I know one thing for sure—no Cheyenne will ever forget what happened today."

Hill pressed, "You checked your rifle?"

"I sure did."

"It's important that you know when to fire—when the exchange is being effected and both prisoners are out in clear view."

"I won't miss him. That Red Shirt ain't going back to his tribe alive, and that's a promise."

"Get going, then." Hill motioned toward a rise opposite the waiting Cheyenne. "That's the perfect spot. You can find yourself enough cover over there so no one will ever know where the shot came from."

"You can count on me, sir. Red Shirt's as good as dead right now."

Wallace spurred his mount into motion.

Watching Wallace's retreating figure until it disappeared from sight, Lieutenant Hill then mumbled in reply, "And no one will ever know where *my* shot came from, Wallace . . . not even you."

A steadfast presence at White Horse's side, Shadow Walker held himself rigidly erect as the approaching military contingent came to a halt, allowing a discreet distance between the opposing delegations. Searching the ranks, Shadow Walker saw Red Shirt mounted tall and proud, and a deep satisfaction registered within him. He then turned his attention to the bearded officer who led the mounted column and assessed him coldly. He saw no resemblance to Miranda in the man's graying hair and dark eyes, nor in the strong features that contrasted so sharply with Miranda's delicate countenance.

The Indian agent familiar to Black Hand approached as Shadow Walker scrutinized Major Thurston more closely.

He saw Thurston scan the Cheyenne force. He noted the moment when Thurston saw Miranda, and he felt the jolt that shook him.

Shadow Walker's jaw locked tight. So, a father would regain a daughter and the Cheyenne would regain a brave warrior—a fair exchange that raised an abrupt, familiar anger within him. Miranda had been his captive, but he knew now that she had never been *his* as he had believed her to be. He had shared his dreams and his heart with her. He had pledged his love and had believed she had done the same—but he had been wrong. He had been unaware of the distance that had remained between them even while she was in his arms—a distance that Miranda had concealed from him.

Forcing his attention back to Tom Edwards as the Indian agent conversed with White Horse in the Cheyenne tongue, Shadow Walker raised his chin with new determination. He had surrendered Miranda to the tribe—a bitter necessity—as bitter as the necessity now to turn her out of his heart.

Sweeping the rear of the military column with his gaze, Private Will Blake turned with a frown toward the youthful soldier riding beside him. Shaking his head, he said, "Sergeant Wallace hasn't returned to the column yet. I don't like this. He said he was going to take a last look around and then join us here. Something's wrong."

"You worry too much, Willy," his fellow trooper responded. "We scouted the whole area like Major Thurston wanted. There wasn't any sign of them Cheyenne trying to pull a fast one. The sarge was just being careful with that last sweep, that's all."

Turning his mount out of the column abruptly, Blake grated, "It's not the Cheyenne I'm worrying about."

"Hey, where are you going?"

The shouted inquiry rang behind him as Blake spurred his mount into a gallop.

Breathing heavily, Lieutenant Hill drew back on his mount's reins in the shadows of a wooded copse. He squinted in the direction of Tom Edwards where the Indian agent continued his conversation with White Horse.

That's it. Keep talking. I need a little more time.

Dismounting, Hill glanced around him, then drew his rifle from its sheath on the saddle. He smiled, aware that at that very moment Wallace was concealed on the hillside opposite him, readying his rifle, too. He enjoyed the thought of the moment to come when the two hostages would meet in neutral territory between the Cheyenne and the military column. The shots would be unexpected—two shots ringing almost simultaneously—coming out of nowhere.

The chaos would be instantaneous when both Red

Shirt *and the girl* fell dead.

Barely controlling his eagerness, Hill raised his rifle to his eye and set his sights on the girl as she and Red Shirt were brought up from the opposing ranks into clear view. Thurston would be devastated by his daughter's death! He would believe the shot was fired by a Cheyenne, for *certainly*, none of his own people would commit such a horrendous deed. Thurston's desire for revenge against the savages would erase forever from his mind any thought about transferring a lieutenant who had done nothing more than warn him about the Cheyenne's barbarism.

His finger on the trigger, Hill watched the exchange with bated breath. White Horse nodded his acceptance of Edwards's words and the girl was released. Riding slowly, she started toward the military contingent as Red Shirt was also released and began riding back to the Cheyenne.

A few more seconds . . . when they were in unrestricted view. . .

An ache inside him deepening to the point of pain, Shadow Walker watched Miranda as the exchange began. Her chin high and her gaze straight ahead, she started toward the military contingent. Glancing across the neutral space, he saw Red Shirt riding toward them, and the pain within became bittersweet.

The two hostages approached each other, their horses' hoofbeats echoing in the strained silence. Shadow Walker watched Miranda's retreating figure—the set of her narrow shoulders, the gleam of her hair, the—

A glint of sunlight on metal flashed in the wooded glade nearby and Shadow Walker was instantly alert. It flashed again, pinpointing the location of a crouched figure concealed there. Shadow Walker saw a rifle raised. From the angle of trajectory, it could be aimed at no one but . . . Miranda!

Spurring his mount forward, Shadow Walker raced into the neutral breach between Miranda and the rifle. Shouts reverberated in the back of his mind as he neared Miranda's side, as he reached for her at the same moment that shots rang out and a hot burst of pain exploded in his back.

The world suddenly slowing around him, Shadow Walker saw Miranda's eyes widen with shocked incredulity when the bullet struck him. The chaos around him droned to a whining din as she was snatched from her horse by a uniformed figure, and Shadow Walker felt himself slipping from his mount to fall heavily into the darkness that claimed him.

CHAPTER EIGHTEEN

"It was all a mistake, Father, a terrible mistake!"

Shaken, Miranda faced her father where he sat behind his desk, his expression grave. Two days had elapsed since that horrendous moment on the wilderness terrain when the world had erupted into the violence and turmoil of gunfire, shouts, and flashing sabers.

Still incredulous, Miranda had relived the stunning events over and over again in her mind. She remembered being brought up from the rear of the Cheyenne contingent to White Horse's side. Refusing to meet Shadow Walker's gaze, unwilling to suffer the accusation she knew she would view there, she had kept her eyes straightforward and her chin high. At a signal from White Horse, she had started toward the military column as Red Shirt had emerged from the soldiers' ranks and started in her direction. She remembered that the silence as Red Shirt and she began the exchange had rung hollowly in her mind.

She wasn't sure what had happened next, except that Shadow Walker had broken from the Cheyenne contingent and started toward her at a gallop. She recalled glimpsing true fear in his eyes the moment before he reached her side—the moment before he was struck by the bullet meant for her.

Everything happened so quickly then. She was snatched off her horse by her father's strong arm and carried back to safety as Shadow Walker fell to the ground, a bloody circle widening on his back. Crying out, she had struggled to be released so she could go to him, but the violent ensuing conflict obscured him from view. Still protesting wildly, she was dragged to the rear of the military ranks and restrained there as the short, turbulent conflict ended abruptly in confused retreat.

Haunting her in the time since was the image of Shadow Walker's limp body being thrown across his mount and carried away by the withdrawing Cheyenne.

Miranda struggled against the lump in her throat that the image evoked. Her father walked around the desk to her side as she rasped, "It shouldn't have happened!"

"But it did, Miranda." His expression pained, Major Thurston brushed a gold strand back from her cheek, continuing softly, "Tom Edwards is already in contact with Black Hand. He thinks it'll be a while before the Cheyenne will trust us enough to parley again."

"But you know the truth now. You can explain that Red Shirt was fired upon by a renegade soldier—that Sergeant Wallace was planning to kill Red Shirt, but Private Blake became suspicious about Wallace's absence from the column and went looking for him—that Private Blake reached Wallace in time to spoil his shot. You can tell the Cheyenne that Sergeant Wallace admitted Lieutenant Hill put him up to it, and Lieutenant Hill will be brought up on charges as soon as he's found."

His bearded jaw hardening, Major Thurston replied, "Hill obviously panicked in the confusion after his shot hit Shadow Walker instead of you. That's the only reason I can figure for the way he inadvertently revealed his location, then took off on the run. Otherwise, it would've been Wallace's word against his. We'll find him, though. There aren't too many places for a man like Hill to hide on the frontier."

"I don't care about Lieutenant Hill." Miranda took a step closer to her father. Grateful when his arms closed around her to hold her comfortingly close, she whispered, "I need to know what happened to Shadow Walker."

Major Thurston's voice grew pained. "He's a Cheyenne, Miranda."

"I won't be able to rest until I know he's all right."

"He's the one who captured you. None of this would've happened if not for him."

"He saved my life."

"But that doesn't change what he did."

"I can't live with not knowing how he is, Father. I . . . we . . ."

Major Thurston's gaze searched hers when Miranda

was unable to continue. Frowning he said, "I'll ask Tom Edwards to make some inquiries. It'll take a while, but he'll find out."

"I need to know *now*."

"I'm sorry, dear."

The finality of her father's tone settled deep inside Miranda. The futility of further protest evident, she left the office without another word.

His world drifting in a haze of weakness and pain, Shadow Walker lay motionless on his sleeping bench. Fragmented memories haunted him: Miranda, mounted solemnly on her horse on the day of the exchange; the glint of a rifle barrel on the wilderness terrain; the realization that the rifle was aimed at Miranda; his mad race to save her—then the impact of the bullet that struck him.

Shadow Walker withheld a pained groan. Rattling Blanket had explained when he awakened later in his lodge that the chaos following the shot had ended in a mutual withdrawal of forces, with Red Shirt escaping to the safety of his Cheyenne brothers, and Miranda being rescued by the horse soldiers.

Safety for Red Shirt. Miranda returned to her people.

Miranda—gone.

The ache within Shadow Walker deepened. Weakness again overwhelming him, he did not realize Two Moons had entered the lodge until her voice penetrated his hazy musings in a tone that betrayed her anxiety as she whispered to Rattling Blanket, "The flames spoke to me again, Rattling Blanket."

Rattling Blanket's efforts to silence Two Moons met with failure as the aged squaw continued, "I saw Spotted Bear in the flames, leaving camp in a jealous rage when our people sorrowed at Shadow Walker's grave wound. I saw him riding, his wrath unrelenting. I saw him dismount to stalk someone in the semi-darkness. Then, as the flames flared, I saw him rise up to sink his blade—to silence forever the spirit of Dancing Star that lives in the blond one's heart!"

"No!"

His protest spontaneous, Shadow Walker fought to clear his clouded mind.

Spotted Bear, stalking Miranda . . .

He struggled to sit up. Ignoring Rattling Blanket's pleas and the blood that began flowing freely from his wound, he drew himself to his feet and started toward the doorway.

Miranda, in danger . . .

His world spinning dangerously, Shadow Walker shook off Rattling Blanket's restraining grip and lurched toward a horse tied up outside the lodge. He gasped with pain as he held the animal fast and attempted to mount.

I must go to her.

Hoisting himself up onto the horse's back at last,

Shadow Walker turned the animal out of camp. He did not feel the blood streaming down his back. Nor did he see the braves running after him, or hear their calls to halt.

Instead, Shadow Walker heard only a thundering in his ears that preceded the darkness which then consumed him.

Dressed in familiar riding attire, Miranda slipped through the night shadows of the fort. Reaching the stable, she untied her saddled mare, then led the animal toward the rear gate. Pausing, she winced at the sight of Private Higgins lying asleep on the ground there. She hadn't liked what she had done. With the pretense of apologizing for her behavior when his patrol was assigned to guard her during the chaos after Shadow Walker was shot, she had brought him a cup of tea heavily laced with sleeping powder taken from the infirmary. Intent on her purpose, she had waited until the fellow had drained the cup dry.

Mounting up, Miranda slipped out through the gate, then pulled it closed behind her. A bright, full moon lighting her way, she traveled the familiar trail cautiously until it faded into the shadowed wilderness terrain. She pressed on, using the stars to guide her.

Fatigue and confusion finally overwhelming her as daylight approached, Miranda dismounted for a few minutes' rest. Shadow Walker's fallen, bloodied image flashed again before her mind as she sat back wearily against a tree. She knew now that the fear she had glimpsed in Shadow

Walker's eyes the moment before the bullet had hit him had been fear for *her* welfare. She knew, because she lived with that same fear.

She had tried to explain how she felt to her father, but he had seemed somehow incapable of understanding the depth of her feelings. She hoped she had made it clear to him in the letter she'd left behind that she knew how dear she was to him, because he was as dear to her—but that she could not rest unless she saw Shadow Walker again. She was certain her father would eventually understand and accept what she had written because she knew his greatest wish was for her happiness.

The unrelenting ache within Miranda deepened. She needed to know Shadow Walker was all right. She needed to talk to him. She needed to say the words she had never said before—that she loved him. She needed to tell him she knew now that the differences between them meant little when the love between them was strong. She needed to say those things, and countless others that crowded her heart.

Battling tears, Miranda took a deep breath. She had no illusions about the many obstacles in the way of locating Shadow Walker. White Horse might have moved his camp; and even if he hadn't, she might not be able to find it. If she did find it, there was no certainty what her reception would be.

She might not survive.

Only one thing was clear. She had to find Shadow Walker. She needed, at least, to try.

Miranda closed her eyes. Exhaustion claiming her, she did not hear the moccasined footsteps approaching. She did not hear them stop beside her. Nor did she hear the knife being drawn from its sheath, or the revealing hiss as it descended swiftly toward her.

Startled awake by the sound of an abrupt, violent scuffle beside her, Miranda jumped to her feet. Her sleep-clouded mind at first failed to comprehend the sight of Cheyenne braves struggling to restrain Spotted Bear—until she saw the knife Spotted Bear still clutched in his hand, and abruptly realized that its blade had been meant for her.

Backing up as the struggle between the braves grew more fierce, Miranda gasped as Spotted Bear wrenched himself free and ran off into the shadows. She heard the sound of his mounted escape as the other braves turned toward her.

The Cheyenne camp lay in the warming rays of the rising sun as squaws emerged from their lodges and made their way down to the stream. Smoke trailed upward from the smoke outlets of the lodges as the young braves of the camp walked to the hillside to gather horses turned out to graze the previous night, signaling that the day had truly begun.

Observing it all from a rise in the distance, Miranda took a shaky breath, then turned to the braves mounted beside her. She saw Standing Elk, Crying Crow, and Buffalo Chaser, the braves who had halted Spotted Bear's knife only inches from her chest. She had listened with throat tight as they told of witnessing Shadow Walker's collapse when he had attempted to ride out to find her, of listening to Running Elk's tale and Two Moons's visions—when they then took up in Shadow Walker's stead and brought her to the spot where she now stood.

With a solemn nod to her rescuers, Miranda nudged her mount into motion. Her heart pounded when she reached the camp and familiar unsmiling faces turned toward her. She saw hostility and suspicion that stopped many in their tracks. She saw the angry advance toward her that halted abruptly when Rattling Blanket stepped into view.

Addressing Rattling Blanket, Miranda said, "Please let me see him."

Standing in the entrance to Shadow Walker's lodge minutes later, Miranda saw Shadow Walker lying on his sleeping bench, his chest wrapped in a bloodstained bandage. His handsome face was pale, but his eyes were clear. He held her fast with his gaze as he waited for her to speak.

Kneeling beside him at last, struggling against deep emotion, Miranda said simply, "I love you, Shadow Walker."

Shadow Walker's arms slipped around her then. His lips were warm against her hair as he rasped words of love in return, and Miranda knew—held passionately in the circle of his embrace—that she was home at last.

AUTHOR'S NOTE

Although based on actual events and characters in American history, MIRANDA AND THE WARRIOR is a fictional story. You won't find Miranda or Shadow Walker mentioned in the history of the American frontier. The appearance of any of my Cheyenne characters' names in your history books is purely coincidental, and although you may find some of the forts I mentioned on the map, Fort Walters is also a fictional fort.

The Cheyenne customs and way of life are authentic, however, as are the flavor, spirit, and excitement of the times.

The conquest of the American West was difficult. We continue to learn from mistakes made on both sides of the conflict, but it was also a romantic time in American history that is uniquely our own. It fascinates, stirs the imagination, and leaves a hunger for more in most people. I hope MIRANDA AND THE WARRIOR has done that for you.

—*Elaine Barbieri*

DEAR READER:

So much intrigue swirls around Miranda and Shadow Walker that it's a wonder their love prevails! But it does, in spite of Spotted Bear and Lieutenant Hill—not to mention Miranda's temper and Shadow Walker's stubbornness.

In May McGoldrick's TESS AND THE HIGHLANDER, two sweethearts are very nearly kept apart by other people's evil intentions as well. When Colin Macpherson washes up on a windswept Scottish isle, he is saved by a mysterious girl living there alone. Colin has always been a bit of a player, with a different girl in every medieval port he passes through, but Tess is different. Colin realizes she means more to him than any lass ever has, but he also discovers her true identity, and that may well keep Tess from him.

Turn the page for an introduction to Tess and her Highlander....

Abby McAden
Editor, Avon True Romance

FROM
TESS AND THE HIGHLANDER
by May McGoldrick

The Isle of May, off the Firth of Forth
Scotland, March 1543

Tess poked at the corpse with a stick and backed away.

Her unbound auburn hair, already soaked from the driving rain, whipped across her eyes when she leaned in to look closer.

The Highlander appeared to be dead, but she couldn't be sure. Long blond hair lay matted across his face. She looked at the high leather boots, darkened by the salt water. The man was wearing a torn shirt that once must have been white. A broad expanse of plaid, pinned at one shoulder by a silver brooch, trailed into the tidal pool. From the thick belt that held his kilt in place, a sheathed dirk banged against an exposed thigh.

A dozen seals watched her from the deep water beyond the surf.

With the storm growing increasingly wilder, she stood

indecisively over the body. In all the years she'd been on the island, she'd never seen a human wash up before. Certainly, there had been wrecks in the storms that swept in across the open water, and Auld Charlotte and Garth used to find all kinds of things—some valuable and some worthless—cast up on the shores. Never, though, had there been another person—at least, not since the aging husband and wife had found Tess herself eleven years earlier.

Tess pushed aside those thoughts now and crouched beside the man, placing a hand hesitantly on his chest. A faint pounding beneath the shirt was the answer to her prayers . . . and her fears. She didn't want anyone intruding on her island and in her life. At the same time, she could not allow a living thing to die when she could save it. Or him.

The surf crashed over the ring of rock that formed the tidal pool, and the young woman pushed herself to her feet. She drew the leather cloak up to shield her face from the stinging spray of wind-driven brine. When she looked back at the body, the wave had pushed the Highlander deeper into the pool, immersing his face.

Tess immediately dropped her stick and lifted his face out of the water. Glancing over her shoulder, she eyed a flat rock at the far side of the pool. It sat higher than the tide generally rose. Rolling him forward slightly, she held him under the arms just as another wave crested the pool's rim. The surge of water lifted the body, and Tess quickly dragged him through the water toward the rock.

He was heavier than she thought he would be. Out of breath, she finally succeeded in getting him partially anchored on the rock.

Auld Charlotte had once told Tess that they'd found her nearly drowned in this same tidal pool. The thought of that now flickered in her mind. She tried to recall the storm and the ship and the day, but those memories had long ago faded into nightmares. Now it was all buried too deeply within her to recollect. She wondered if it had been a day like this one.

The dirk at the Highlander's side caught her eye, and Tess reached down quickly, yanked the weapon from its sheath, and tucked it into her own belt.

The wind was howling, and the salt spray was stinging her face. Tess looked out at the frothy, gray-green sea, hoping to see some boat searching for the Highlander lying unconscious beside her.

If they came, she wouldn't let herself be seen, though. She wanted no news of her presence to be carried to the mainland.

She had been only six years old when the ship had sunk and she had washed ashore. But the little she allowed herself to remember from the time before that day was too painful. Tess had no desire to face that horrifying past ever again. There was no place else that she ever wanted to be but here. This island was the only home she had left.

For eleven years the reclusive couple had kept her exis-
tence a secret. And now, with both of them dead, she
could only pray to continue her life as before, undisturbed.

Her plan was the same as the one she'd followed
dozens of times since washing up on this island. Whenever
there was a chance of a fishing boat or some pilgrims coming ashore, Garth and Charlotte would trundle Tess off
with plenty of food and blankets to the caves on the western shore of the island. She would remain there in safety
until all was well and the visitors were gone.

The only difference now was that she would have to
use her own judgment about when it would be safe to
come out.

Ready to push herself to her feet, Tess felt a tinge of
curiosity that made her reach out and push the Highlander's wet hair out of his face. Instantly she was sorry for
the action, for the man's features took her by surprise. Even
unconscious, or perhaps because of it, he was an extremely
handsome man. A high forehead, a straight nose, a face
devoid of the beard that she'd assumed all Highlanders
wore. He had a face not even marred by scars . . . yet. Only
a few scratches and bruises from his time in the surf.

Angry for allowing herself to be distracted, she started
to get to her feet, but one foot slipped, and she had to
brace a hand on his chest to catch herself.

His eyes immediately opened, and Tess's breath
knotted tightly in her chest. Blue eyes the color of a

winter sky stared at her from beneath long dark lashes flecked with gold. She didn't blink. She didn't move. Holding her breath, she remained still for the eternity of a moment until he closed them again.

She edged off the rock and ran as fast and as far as her legs would take her.

The taste in Colin Macpherson's mouth was foul as a dried-up chamber bucket.

Rolling onto his side, he felt his stomach heave. He tried to push himself up. He couldn't see. As he turned, Colin's hand slipped off cold wet rock, and he tumbled into a shallow pool of water, banging his ribs hard on the stone as he fell.

"Blasted hell." He groaned, pushing himself onto his knees. Holding his head, he blinked a few times, trying to clean the sand and salt out of his eyes.

Rocks. More rocks. And water. And bobbing heads. He pushed back a long, twisted hank of hair that had fallen across his face, obstructing his vision. He tried to focus on the creatures moving on the rocks.

Seals—a dozen or so—were staring at him from the rocks rimming the pool and from the sea beyond. Their brown eyes were dark and watchful. The image of a woman's face immediately flashed before his mind, and he struggled to push himself to his feet. A couple of seals barked a warning to those on shore.

"H-hullo!" he called out, only to have the surf and the wind slap the greeting back into his face.

His entire body ached. It had taken great effort to get the words out past his raw, scratched throat, but Colin tried again. He was certain someone had been there only moments before. Or was it hours?

"Hullo!"

This time the shriek of seabirds was his only answer. Taking in a painful half breath, he tried to move his feet in the shallow pool. They moved, though it felt as if they were made of lead. Colin succeeded in taking only three steps before he had to sit down on the edge of a rock. The world was spinning around in his head.

Water. Rocks. And on each side of the protected tidal pool, rock-studded banks dotted with occasional patches of sea grass sloped upward from the turbulent sea.

The Macpherson ship had been sailing north when the weather had taken a turn for the worse. It shouldn't have been unexpected, though. The Firth of Forth was famous for its foul and quickly changing moods.

Half o'er, half o'er, from Aberdour. It's fifty fathom deep. And there lies good Sir Patrick Spence, with the Scots lords at his feet. Well, Colin thought, at least he had washed ashore . . . wherever he was.

The last clear memory that Colin had was of shoving one of the sailors to safety in the aft passageway. The lad was nearly unconscious after being slammed against the ship's gunwales as the great vessel had continued to heel before the tempestuous blast of wind.

The storm had come on fast and hard, but they'd been riding it well. Colin and Alexander, his eldest brother, had been standing with the second mate at the tiller when he'd seen the young man go down. The sea sweeping across the deck had nearly carried the lad overboard.

Colin fought the urge to be ill. The foul, salty taste rose again into his mouth.

The lad had no sooner been secured when Colin had heard the cries of the lookout above. The dark shape of land appeared, not an arrowshot to port. And then the ship's keel had struck the sandbar.

He remembered being bounced hard across the deck, only to have the sea lift him before plunging him deep into the brine. After a lifetime thrashing in the dark waters, he'd finally sputtered to the surface. All he'd heard then was the howling shriek of the wind before another crashing wall of water drove him under again. Somehow he'd survived it all, though he had no idea how.

He stared again at a seal, who was watching him intently. For an insane moment, thoughts of legends told by sailors clouded his reason.

A gust of cold wind blasting mercilessly across the stormy water instantly sobered him. He was soaked through and chilled to the bone. Colin managed to push himself to his feet and climb out of the tidal pool.

Another image of dark eyes looking down at him

flashed through his mind. The eyes of a young woman. He remembered more now. Someone pulling him through the water. Propping him on the rock. She had been no apparition. Colin braced himself against the wind and let his gaze sweep over his surroundings.

"Where are you?" he shouted over the wind. There was not a boat or person, not even a tree in sight, and the rising slope of rocky ground straight ahead hampered Colin's vision of what lay beyond.

"And where am I?" he muttered to himself.